ARABESQUE

ARABESQUE

COLIN MULHERN

Catnip

For Paula

CATNIP BOOKS
Published by Catnip Publishing Ltd
14 Greville Street
London EC1N 8SB

This edition first published 2012
1 3 5 7 9 10 8 6 4 2

Text © 2012 Colin Mulhern
The moral right of the author has been asserted.

A CIP catalogue record for this book is available from the British Library.

ISBN 978-1-84647-148-3

Printed in India

www.catnippublishing.co.uk

'Teenage girls have an annoying habit of thinking for themselves.'

Be the best.

It was a philosophy her dad had taught her. Her mother might have been content that Amy was healthy, happy, comfortable and doing well, but there were occasions when her dad would check that they were alone and quietly say, 'Sometimes, Amy, there's no prize for second place. Do you know what I mean?'

Amy would look away with a disapproving scowl. She understood exactly what he meant: second best in certain situations meant being killed.

But her dad would reach out a hand, touch her cheek and gently encourage her to meet his eyes. 'Hey, don't go there. I'm talking about you. Whatever you do in life. Don't be content with second place. Put the work in. Be the *best*.'

And even though she hated him saying it, hated *why* he said it, the words had stuck. She became obsessive about it, which was why she was on course for a string of top grades, and why, on a Saturday morning, most eyes in the gymnasium were on Amy May.

The place was nothing special. The floor was scratched and pockmarked. The crash mats were worn. The wooden wall bars were usable, but they could do with a new coat of varnish. It was just an average school gym, holding itself together and doing its best to fit the needs of enthusiastic, amateur gymnasts.

Despite its run-down appearance, the gymnasium was in high demand, so much so that different age groups worked alongside each other. The coaches taking five- and six-year-old beginners encouraged basic moves and balances, while others pushed teenagers to perfection. Around the gymnasium, on plastic chairs and unused or damaged benches, parents of the younger years chatted, occasionally applauding and nudging each other.

As Amy and her partner were warming up, stretching muscles, working joints and ligaments, one parent gave a whoop and flashed a camera.

Mia rolled her eyes. 'If there's one thing I cannot stand, it's sickly sweet parents.'

Amy smiled. 'You always say that on Saturdays.'

'Because they're worse on weekends. Constantly waving, clapping their hands at a forward roll.'

'You were there once, Mia.'

'I didn't bring the whole family with me! Look at them. It's not like the kids are going to wander off. Why don't they leave them and go shopping for an hour or something?'

Amy laughed. 'They want to watch. Why do you have such a problem with that?'

'I don't have a problem.'

'Every time a parent claps you twist your face.'

'I don't.'

'Mia, you do it if they even nod appreciatively.'

They turned to face each other, ready to go through a routine they had been developing for the past few weeks.

Mia raised her arms. 'It doesn't do them any good. Praise should be used with care.'

'You prefer the stick rather than the carrot, do you?'

'Damn right. You can't coax a donkey to move with a carrot unless it's hungry. Hit the beast with a big enough stick . . .' Mia jumped forward and whirled round, her leg shooting out in a smooth, flying roundhouse kick.

Amy ducked and sidestepped with ease. 'You're getting better, but not good enough, Mia. If you want to use the stick on me, you'll have to be a lot faster than that.'

Mia padded from foot to foot, hands held up like she was ready to fight. 'Which is a perfect argument in my favour. Independence tightens reactions. If you pamper a child with kisses and cuddles over every little thing, they'll stay slow and lazy.'

'Rubbish,' said Amy. 'I've only ever got praise. No one used a stick on me.'

'You are your own stick.'

Amy considered and nodded. 'A mix of both. Which is why . . .' She made to lunge, her right hand balled into a tight fist. Mia dodged to one side only to take a smack from Amy's left hand. '. . . I am a lot faster than you.'

'Girls!' The powerful voice of a squat, chunky female coach shook the gym. 'Stop messing about. Finish your warm up and get started.'

Mia waited until the coach had turned, then tried to catch Amy with a kick to her calf, but again Amy was too fast, so Mia went back to the argument. 'Half of them don't even watch their kids. You know as much as I do why they really hang about. Who most of them are looking at.'

Amy tried to mask a small smile. 'Well. If that's the case, I might as well show them something worthwhile.'

Stubbs was in a whirl of panic. His flat was a mess, but that was standard; he had slept in his clothes and needed a shave, but that wasn't so unusual either. What worried him was the empty bed in the spare room and the wide-open front door.

He paused as he approached the battered old sofa where Micky Carlisle lay grunting in his sleep. Here was a monster of a man with huge, tattooed arms folded across his chest and grey combat trousers tucked into enormous, black paratrooper boots, each with a line of studs in the side to make them extra mean. Everything was calculated to reinforce the image of a mercenary.

He was lying with his nose pressed against a cushion, causing his top lip to curl into a silent snarl.

Even at rest, Micky looked angry.

Stubbs took a deep breath and carefully shook him by the shoulder.

The man on the sofa instantly recoiled. He sniffed in a sharp breath, squinted and looked up. 'What's going on?'

Stubbs felt ill enough – head pounding, dehydration, as well as the lingering disorientation of a serious hangover – but that was small-time compared to the knot of terror tightening in his gut at what he had to say to Micky, so he started gently. 'I think we both passed out.'

'Mmm?'

On the coffee table, among the debris of beer cans, pizza boxes and crisp packets, were two empty bottles of tequila. Stubbs grabbed one. 'Remember this?'

Micky rubbed his face. 'Yeah. So?'

Stubbs's voice was shaking so much he had to push the words out. 'You don't think Maurice was unusually generous last night? All that, "Come on boys, the deal's as good as done – celebrate! Knock it back." You didn't find that odd?'

'What are you going on about? What time is it?'

Stubbs swallowed. 'He's gone. Maurice. He's done a runner.'

'What?'

'I'm not kidding. Maurice is gone. And so is the money.'

Micky was up and on his feet in an instant. 'He's taken it?'

Stubbs took a step backwards. 'That's what it looks like. His car's not there, and the stuff from his room: his bag, his laptop . . . all gone.'

Micky snatched the empty bottle from Stubbs's hands, gave it a quick, disbelieving look, then slung it to the far side of the room. It shattered with a crash.

His voice was low. 'I don't believe this.'

Stubbs retreated another few steps, giving Micky space.

It was just as well. Micky let out a scream of rage and kicked the coffee table flying.

'I'll kill him!' he cried. 'I'll bloody kill him.'

Stubbs backed up to the corner, nervously watching while Micky glared about the room. He felt his stomach go weak as Micky's eyes locked on the television. The TV was basic, almost worthless, but it was his, and he didn't want it going out of the window like his stereo had three weeks ago – just because a CD had dared to skip a few times.

Thinking quickly, Stubbs grabbed his mobile phone. 'We can call him.'

Micky went directly for the television, growling curses.

'Look! I'll call him now.' Stubbs pushed the speed-dial just as Micky reached out towards the TV . . .

. . . and grabbed the pack of cigarettes from the top.

'Anything?' he asked, turning round and lighting up.

Stubbs could feel the sweat on his palm against the back of the mobile as he listened for a tone. 'It's turned off,' he said.

Micky looked ready to explode and Stubbs was worried that being the only other living soul in the flat, he might bear the brunt of it. He quickly added, 'I'll send him a text.'

But Micky shook his head. 'No point. He's not going to respond, is he?' He sat back down on the sofa. 'This can't be happening.' Staring at the floor, he slowly shook his head. 'This *cannot* be happening.'

'So what do we do?' said Stubbs. 'Cancel the whole thing?'

Micky took a drag on his cigarette, blowing the smoke out through his nose. 'No chance. Not with these people . . . If they even *suspect* we're messing them about, they'll kill us. You, me . . . even Carla. They'll kill all of us. Simple as that.'

'Yeah, but if we haven't got the money . . .'

'We *find* the money.'

'You mean we go after Maurice?'

Micky paused, then shook his head. 'He knows me too well; knows what I'll do. If Maurice has ripped us off, he'll be on a plane somewhere by now.'

'So what do we do?'

Micky Carlisle looked. 'We find some *more* money.'

'What? Twenty grand? In a day? Even if we had a whole week, and I could ring enough cars, we don't have Maurice to sell them on.'

'I don't care. We have to find the money.'

'But . . . but . . . twenty grand? That's twenty *thousand* pounds. What the hell are we going to d—'

'Shut your mouth and sit down!' Micky took another deep drag on his cigarette. 'I'm thinking.'

At 10:04am, on that same Saturday morning, Carla sent the text message that would kill her.

She hadn't been surprised when she'd woken alone. Micky often stayed at Stubbs's flat, and that was fine by her. Personally, she liked the comforts of her own house. Well, technically it wasn't her *own* house; it was rented from family. A harmless scam that gave her parents a house-sitter and allowed her to keep the housing benefit. Whatever. The important thing was that she preferred the comforts of a decent semi in a good area to the squalid little flat where Stubbs lived. And she would much rather Micky stayed there with him, rather than bring that horrible little man here. Stubbs was an idiot – gifted at ringing cars, but an idiot all the same.

Maurice was different. He was the opposite of Stubbs. He was always well turned out, always shirts and trousers, never T-shirt and jeans. He thought he was a cut above, choosing to carry a briefcase, to wear a tie. But it worked. And it was Maurice who had come up with the original plan.

* * *

Maurice had got them all together just over a month ago, rubbing his hands like an over-excited schoolboy, asking them all to take a seat because he had a major announcement.

Finally, he'd said, 'Guns.' He smiled broadly, nodding at them. 'Guns and ammunition.' They had looked at him like he was mad, but he pushed on. 'This could be the turning point for us. We can make some *real* money for a change. I'm telling you. If we can find the money to invest, we buy a small consignment and sell it on.'

'Sell it?' Micky asked.

'I've got a buyer lined up. Several buyers, which means we can go with the highest price.'

Carla pulled Micky aside. 'Do you actually trust him on this? This is a big jump from stealing cars.'

But her boyfriend ignored her. 'What's the cut?'

Furious at being snubbed, Carla spoke directly to Maurice. 'Hold on a moment. Why can't these buyers just go straight to the person you're buying from?'

'Because we're buying bulk,' was the simple answer. 'This man imports the guns and shifts them to distributors for a quick turnaround, but also to keep himself one step removed from the criminals who want the stock. It's down to the distributors to sell them on to anyone who wants them, which is why the distributors can make so much money. In this case, we become a distributor – the link in the chain – and we'll make a fortune. We could easily double our investment.'

Carla still didn't like it. She cut to the quick. 'How much are we talking about?'

'Twenty grand.' Maurice sat back, folded his arms and waited for a response.

Stubbs gave a quiet, 'Woah.'

Carla snorted. 'You're joking. We don't have that kind of money.'

But Micky saw pound signs. 'Are you serious? We could double it?'

'Pretty much. I can give you the exact figures later, but this is a sweet, sweet, deal.'

'Yes,' agreed Carla, '*if* we happened to have the money. Unfortunately—'

Maurice cut her off. 'We've got about four weeks. I've got some money stashed, and I know for a fact you and Micky have. We can make up the difference. I've already worked it out. This is not beyond us. We've just got to think of the bigger picture. Move beyond petty crime and do something professional for a change.'

Stubbs looked as blank as ever, but Micky was smiling and nodding. 'I like the sound of that: "professional".' He clapped a hand on Carla's thigh. 'What do you say? Time to move up in the world? It might be a way for us to get a place like this, or something even better, eh?'

Carla felt boxed in. On the one hand, it seemed too big a risk, but on the other, the idea of moving away from petty crime, away from just getting by, to transform themselves from low-life thieves and scroungers into a black market distribution business. Well . . . it certainly had its merits. And maybe if Micky believed it . . .

'Okay,' she said. 'Count me in.'

Within hours, Maurice had set the wheels in motion. And throughout the next four weeks, her doubts turned into hope as the money began to mount up. They worked tooth and nail, pulled the money from every conceivable scam and hustle. And yesterday, with three days to go, it was looking like their efforts had paid off.

Maurice gathered them together at Stubbs's flat for a final talk. All of the money was there, everything accounted for.

'I've counted it twice.' With care, he began to place the bundles of cash into his open briefcase. 'What you are looking at is just over twenty-two thousand pounds.' He took out two twenty pound notes. 'We have the option to buy more stock if we have the cash, but I think we deserve a well earned pat on the back.' He looked at them with a smile. 'What do you say? Pizza, or Chinese?'

'I say we could do with it,' said Micky.

Maurice held up a hand. 'I hope you don't mind, but I took the liberty of using a few notes to buy us a little something for a celebration.' He placed two bottles of tequila on the table.

Micky's eyes lit up. 'Nice one.' He had the top off in a second, leaning towards Carla. 'Go get some glasses, love.'

Carla put a taunting finger to her chin. 'Hmm, let me think. Tequila, pizza and a game of cards.' She held up her hands. 'Sorry, boys. Not quite my scene.' She gave

Micky a kiss. 'If you come home drunk, try not to make too much noise.'

When she woke up this morning and realised Micky hadn't made it home, she had a pretty good idea just how drunk they'd all been.

Still, in two days they were going to do the deal of a lifetime. They were allowed a small celebration.

At 9:52, a text appeared on her phone.

I'm not getting a reply from M. Are we on?

There was no caller ID, but Carla knew exactly who it was from. Andy Galloway had demanded contact numbers for every member of the team – but his primary contact was Maurice.

Carla shrugged. Maurice was probably flat out asleep with the other two. Besides, this was the agreed address, so why should he have all the glory? They were supposed to be a team. They had found the cash as a team, they were doing the deal as a team. If Maurice wasn't sober enough to turn his phone on, then Carla had no choice but take control. Her reply was a simple:

The money is ready when you are.

The screen flashed a brief confirmation before melting back to a photo: a self portrait, taken at arm's length. Carla and Micky. Cheeks pressed together to fit into the frame. Laughing. Happy.

GYMNASIUM
SOUTHFIELD SCHOOL

It was around this time that Amy May was in the school gymnasium, defying gravity on the uneven bars. A straddle-back from the top, to a handstand on the lower bar had every parent in that gym hypnotised, fantasising that one day their own child could manage something equally incredible. The majority had read the local news feature on her. For those who hadn't, it was pinned to the notice board in the entrance hall.

FLIPPING MARVELLOUS

Amy May is back-flipping her way to the top. At 15 years old she has enough trophies to fill her own display cabinet and is well on the road to national success. Currently training for the Junior British Championship, Amy, of Brookfield, insists there is no big secret to her success.

'It's pure hard work,' Amy told us. 'I'm nothing special. I just put in a lot of time and practice.'

But it's not all work and no play. Both Amy and her training partner make sure they leave time for fun.

'We do a few hours at the gym,' explained Amy, 'then we go over to the shopping centre and meet up with other friends. We shop, we eat burgers, then go bowling or see a movie.'

And although Amy insists she's just like any other teenager, her coach, Laura Barnes, disagrees.

'Every athlete puts in hard work. It's essential. But every now and then, someone comes along who makes you sit up. There's no other way to put it. Amy May has the X-Factor.'

And how does Laura feel about Amy missing this year's Olympics?

'Gutted. But she's fifteen and rules are rules. All I'm thinking about right now is Amy's routines for the championships. She is currently perfecting four: vault, uneven bars, beam and floor. Without being cocky about it, Amy could wipe the board. She's that good.'

A spokesperson of events organisers, British Gymnastics, said, 'We keep a careful eye on the Junior Championships. Gymnasts who do well at that level are often heading towards Olympic Gold.'

Perhaps if the article hadn't been published, Amy's day might have turned out differently. Perhaps she would have made it to the shopping centre, ordered a burger, spent the afternoon shopping.

But the article *had* been published, and to everyone who had picked up the local paper that day, Amy May was someone special.

FIX-FAST DIY
TOWN CENTRE

Stubbs had a talent for acquiring vehicles. It was this skill, along with Maurice's ability to sell the same vehicles on, that had allowed them to build up the money.

This final job was short notice, but Micky had expressed just how important it was.

'We need a van. And we need it quick.'

Stubbs wasn't happy, but he wasn't up to arguing either. Instead, he went out and got to work.

Working in the day wasn't a problem, in fact, it was his preference. His usual time was around ten in the morning, just when car owners were in the office, having a morning cuppa, reading a paper, and not for a moment suspecting that their vehicle could be in danger.

Stubbs had several pairs of overalls – all different colours, with different logos on the back: "Dean's Auto Repairs", "MEK-A-NIX", "Car Glass" and "North East Locksmiths". The idea was simple – a dark figure huddled next to a car at three in the morning reeked of suspicion, but a guy in overalls in broad daylight was as good as invisible. To remain invisible, he never used the same overalls in the same car park, or at least not within a good few months of his last visit.

Today, he wore a dark red tunic and trousers with a peaked cap of the same colour. There was a logo on his breast pocket and his tool box only added authenticity.

The tools of his trade were simple, but effective. There was no breaking glass, no forcing of locks – in fact, no damage at all. Stubbs took pride in the fact that the cars he passed on to Maurice were ready for sale. No repairs, no touch ups – just a quick change of plates and a price tag.

But not today.

Today, his need for a vehicle was driven by a different motivation and, according to his instructions, the plain white Transit van parked near the main entrance of a DIY shop was perfect.

He walked up to the driver's door, placed his toolbox on the ground and opened it. Several people walked past as Stubbs got to work, first examining the lock, then checking the contents of his case. Some crossed in front of the van, some behind, but none of them seemed to take much notice as Stubbs straightened up, slipped a thin length of metal down the side of the window, unlocked the mechanism from within and opened the van's door.

And no one suspected anything as, a moment later, he started the engine and drove away.

CORRIDOR
SOUTHFIELD SCHOOL

Tired but glowing, with bags slung over their shoulders, Amy and Mia made their way out of the changing rooms, passing by the open gymnasium doors. Routine music from large, outdated speakers mixed with the shouts of coaches and the clapping hands of doting parents.

Mia rolled her eyes. Amy just shook her head and with a short laugh said, 'Don't.'

They passed toilet doors and notice boards, and were just approaching a turn in the corridor, when a figure stepped out in front of them. A woman, heavy-set with glasses and hair like straw.

Thinking it was just another parent, Amy shifted to one side, but when the figure matched her, she came to a standstill.

'Amy May?'

Amy hitched up her bag. 'Yes.'

The woman fumbled in a pocket and pulled out a notepad. 'You look shattered. I suppose you're putting in an awful lot of hours at the moment.' Then she shook her head in a way that looked entirely false and said,

'Sorry. Pam Barker,' she tucked the notepad under her arm and held out a hand. 'From the *Echo*.'

From around the same corner, a man appeared. He looked like a mechanic or something, in red overalls and a cap. He seemed to forget something, turned tail and disappeared.

The woman didn't notice him. Instead, she checked her notepad and tried to make out she didn't know where to begin. 'I suppose you're getting quite a bit of this right now: the eyes of the world and all that.'

'Well, not quite,' replied Amy. 'But I already did an interview for you. It was just two weeks back. A young girl called . . .'

'Malorie. Yes. And that was great. We got a fantastic response too. I mean, someone from our own town getting ready to take on the best in the country.'

Amy finally relaxed and allowed herself a small smile. 'Well, I'm not exactly there yet.'

'No? According to the rumour mill you're a sure bet. I caught a bit of your training back there. Incredible stuff.'

Beside Amy, Mia put her weight on one leg and folded her arms.

Very quickly, the woman added, 'Oh, and is this your training partner?'

With a sarcastic wave, Mia said, 'Yeah, that's me. The shadow.'

Amy caught this, laughed and gave her a nudge. 'She's a bit more than that. Keeps me going. We bounce ideas about. She—'

'Yeah, fantastic. But back to you, Amy. With your father so rarely at home, do you worry that he's not going to be there to support you?'

Amy's eyes narrowed. 'What?'

'It's just, we thought we might make a feature of sport bringing families together.'

'Don't give me that,' said Amy. 'Your colleague tried the same thing. She kept asking question after question, then got all narked because I wouldn't tell her what my dad does for a living. I'll tell you what I told her: it's none of your damn business. And just to clear it up once and for all: my parents are *not* separated. If my dad can be there, he will. End of!'

Micky sat in the passenger seat of the recently stolen white van. The van had undergone one slight modification, and from just a few feet away, the blacked-out rear windows looked every bit the professional job. It would take a real nosy parker to realise the effect had been achieved with cut-up bin liners and black electrician's tape. Micky checked his watch. Why was Stubbs taking so long?

'Hurry up,' he whispered.

Stubbs appeared at the far end of the car park, walking quickly towards the van. He ran the last few steps and opened the driver's door.

'Well,' demanded Micky. 'Did you see her?'

Stubbs nodded. 'I think so. There's two girls talking to some local journalist.'

'Be sure.' Micky handed over his phone where he'd Googled for a picture of the North East's star gymnast. It hadn't been hard.

'Yeah. That's one of them, only problem is, she's got a friend with her.'

'I thought she might. I read all about her in the newspaper last week. She tries to come across like she's a regular kid, but I know a few things about Amy May that the newspaper failed to mention.'

'Like what?'

Micky sniffed and adjusted his seating. 'I used to work for a bloke a few years back, doing driveways – block paving. You know what I mean? All fiddle work of course. I was on job-seeker's and the gaffer was getting cheap labour. Everyone a winner, eh? Well anyway, the first jobs I worked on were all in Brookfield.'

'Brookfield?'

'It's an estate up past the hospital. All private, but it's only small. Local newspapers always like to say where people are from, don't they? So when I read she was from Brookfield, it caught my attention. I looked at the picture again and something clicked.

'Some of the houses up there are like mansions, but there was one with this massive driveway. Took us forever. The woman was real snotty – asking how long we'd be, when she'd be able to park her car on the drive, saying she didn't like it left on the road. I wasn't surprised. It was a monstrous, big, executive thing. Must have cost a fortune. Anyway, while we worked, there was a little girl, just as snotty as her mother, asking us this, asking us that, doing handstands and cartwheels and back-flips on the lawn. She was just a bairn, but she was good, you know? Like, *really* good. So when I saw the picture in the paper, it all came back. That was her.'

Stubbs looked blank. 'Which means?'

'Which *means* her mother is probably still loaded. A house like that will be worth nearly a million these days. But you know what really wound me up?'

'What?'

'In all the time it took to do that driveway, she never made us a single cup of tea. Sounds petty, I know. But when you're working all day to make her house look better, it isn't a lot to ask, is it?'

'You think she'll pay up?' Stubbs began drumming his hands on the dashboard.

Micky looked at Stubbs's hands. When they stopped tapping, he looked at Stubbs himself. 'You got a problem with this?'

Stubbs inhaled deeply. 'What? No. Well, not really. I'm just . . . What I mean is, this is pretty heavy stuff, Micky. We're talking kidnap and extortion. Wouldn't it be easier to rob a shop?'

'How many would we have to do to get twenty grand?'

'A bank then?'

'With two of us? Get real. You pull a gun in a bank, they'll send in a squad of armed police. Tear gas, flash bangs, the works. But extortion . . . Do you know the strategy the police have in dealing with kidnap demands?'

'No.'

'Pay the ransom!' He let the words hang for a moment, then sat back, eyes on the building, where the doors opened and two teenage girls walked out.

'What about her friend?' asked Stubbs.

'All part of the plan,' replied Micky. His tone was cold and to the point. 'We need them both.'

CAR PARK
SOUTHFIELD SCHOOL

Amy and Mia walked through the main doors into the noon sunlight of a perfectly pleasant day. The sky was streaked with a few wisps of white cloud, and the breeze was cool. It was warm, it was bright, and so much better than getting the bus. After the artificial lights, the echoes and noise of the gymnasium, it was good to be outside, to walk, to chat. And the shopping centre was only a mile away. Hardly any distance at all.

As the girls walked out of the school gates onto the main road, neither noticed the white van slowly drive past.

'Dan's meeting us later,' said Mia.

'He's not!'

'And he's bringing a friend.'

'I'm not interested.'

'You haven't even seen him.'

'I don't want to. Look, Mia, if you're happy with Dan, then I'm happy for you, but the last thing I need is a boyfriend.'

'Who said anything about a *boy*friend? Why do you think I call him Dan the Man?'

'Oh great – and there goes my appetite, right there.'

Pulling out her mobile, Mia ran ahead. 'You want me to text him? Tell him how excited you are?'

Amy gave chase and grabbed for the phone. 'Don't you dare!'

Arguing and laughing, the two very nearly ran into the man up ahead.

'Er, do you two know if there's a school around here?'

Amy looked up. What kind of idiot couldn't find the school?

The man was standing by a white Transit van. The back door was open and he appeared to be having serious trouble making sense of a map.

'It's just behind us,' said Mia, using her phone to point in the direction they'd come from. 'About five minutes that way.'

The man stood up, but he kept his face down, like he was totally locked on the map. The peak of his cap completely shadowed his face.

'I can't make head nor tail of these directions. You sure it's not over there?'

Amy got a tiny spark of suspicion. There was something wrong here. A van driver without a sat nav or phone? And there was something familiar about the man – his red tunic, trousers and that cap. He was looking entirely the wrong way, pointing in the direction the girls were headed, but at the same time, he was holding his sheet of directions out . . . like he was offering it.

She couldn't help reaching out . . .

And then a sound behind her: a series of footsteps,

quick and heavy. Instinct took over. Amy turned, only to see a shadow as a cloth bag was thrust over her head. She tried to grab it, but arms clamped around her and a voice in her ear hissed, 'Don't move, girl. Don't you dare struggle.'

Right next to her, she heard Mia scream, but the sound was muffled. The scream was followed by a crack and a clatter – Mia's phone!

Ignoring the warning, Amy *did* struggle. She twisted, trying to crouch down to get free. But the arms held her tighter. Escape was impossible, so she screamed, twisting her head from left to right.

Immediately, she was pulled violently to one side, picked up and thrown forward. When she hit the hard surface, she knew she was inside the van.

A man's voice, 'Get the other one in,' was followed by another muffled cry from Mia, and Amy felt the weight of her friend being thrown alongside her. One of the men clambered inside the van, making it shake, and a voice growled, 'Keep your mouth shut. Scream again and I'll knock you unconscious.'

The van doors slammed closed, but the man was inside with them. Amy could hear him fiddling about, then she felt a hard yank on her hands, pulling them together.

'Hold still.'

Something slipped over her hands, onto her wrists. A cable tie. Just before it zipped up, Amy tensed her muscles as hard as she possibly could. Her fists were locked as the plastic tie cut into her skin.

The van wobbled again as up in front, the other man

climbed into the driver's seat and slammed the door.

Beside Amy, Mia screamed, '*Let me go!*'

The reply was immediate and thick with threat. 'I told you to keep quiet, girl.' There was a thump, a short yell from Mia and the man added, 'Keep your hands still, or I swear, I'll break them.'

This was followed by the clear zipping sound of another cable tie.

The van's engine started up.

Amy's mind was spinning. What was going on? *Why* was it going on? Who were these people?

She twisted and pulled against the cable tie. A hand gripped her upper arm, the full weight of that man pressing down. 'Don't try it. You understand me? You're not going anywhere until I say, so keep still and keep quiet. Both of you. We're going for a little drive, and you're both going to keep still and very, very quiet.'

Amy felt herself rock slightly as the van pulled away, and she could feel Mia shaking next to her, sobbing, saying over and over, 'We haven't done anything. We haven't done a thing.'

'I said SHUT UP.'

Amy felt the clunk of the van's gears, but there was no racing engine, no screech of tyres, just calm, sensible driving and the heavy breath of the man beside her.

For some reason, that made it all the more unnerving.

Every instinct in her body was telling Amy to scream and shout and struggle and do whatever it took to get out of this van. Her heart was going crazy and her head was thumping, but somehow she found the will power to fight the panic, to calm down and focus. She could almost hear her father's voice, his stories, tales of impossible situations . . .

She checked the ties on her wrists. Tensing up had worked – when she relaxed, she could feel the cable tie move. It wasn't as tight as it should have been. *Good*, but she couldn't act on it yet. The man who grabbed her was right next to them. She couldn't see him because of the stupid bag on her head, but she had no doubt that he could see every move she made. Amy was certain of two things: he was dangerous and he knew what he was doing. The fact that he'd dared to grab them at all confirmed the first, but that he'd done it so quickly and effectively made her realise the truth of the second. She hadn't even had a chance to turn. She hadn't seen his face, or that of his accomplice – the man with the cap, the man she assumed was now driving the van. But there was another point: the man who'd grabbed her was incredibly strong. Amy was slim, but working out five days a week meant she was solid muscle. This guy had lifted her up like she was made of paper.

She had to keep control, stay calm and think.

Okay, so what *could* she do?

Her father's words came to her: 'You become a zombie. You give nothing, ask nothing, and respond like you're pumped full of tranquilisers.'

So she tried her best. She relaxed and let her body go limp. Slowing her breathing was a little harder, her body was fuelled with adrenalin and right next to her, Mia was sobbing. Every now and then she'd cry out,

'Why are you doing this? Who are you? What do you want with us?'

As Mia began to fall apart, Amy battled with her own fears to keep calm, to relax.

The van slowed, swung to the left, and then immediately to the right. A roundabout. They must be going around a roundabout.

Amy used the sway of the van to shift closer to Mia.

Mia cried out, 'Let us go! Both of us. Right now!'

The answer was all the more terrifying for sounding so calm. 'Shut your mouth, little girl, or I might have to shut it for you.'

Amy shifted until she could hear her friend's breathing.

She whispered as quietly as she dared. 'Keep quiet, Mia. Please. Don't wind him up.'

There was another sob, giving Amy hope that Mia had heard.

'We're going to get out of this if you keep calm. You understand me? I promise. We're going to be okay.' She had to stop to take a breath. With the sack on her head, breathing was laboured and hot. 'Bite your teeth twice if you understand me.'

There was a pause, and then Amy felt, more than heard: click-click.

'Whatever you do,' whispered Amy, 'don't get him – don't get *either* of them – angry. Just stay calm.' She paused. What more could she say? Best to keep it simple.

'I've got an idea.'

WHITE VAN
ON THE MOVE

Micky Carlisle sat in the back of the van, his back against the wall, legs stretched out in front of him. The van stunk to high heaven. The smell of window putty and paint, and God-knows-what else, was rank. But it was satisfaction, not disgust, which made his top lip curl, content in his ability to control the situation.

One of the girls hadn't said a word – probably terrified out of her wits, but the other – the one with the pink flash on her trainers – had screamed and cried for a bit. He needed her to shut up, and a few light threats did the trick. Good – if they were scared, they wouldn't give him any trouble and this whole mess could be cleared up quickly. Get things back on course.

He tried working out what the difference would be with Maurice out of the picture, what sort of cut he would get, but he couldn't make sense of the figures.

Ah, who cared? The important thing was that the cut would be better.

He craned his neck, trying to see through to the windscreen. 'How we doing?'

'Nearly there,' called back Stubbs.

Micky nodded to himself, more confident than ever that he had just saved his own skin. Stubbs and Carla's too, for that matter. It had been a close shave but that money was as good as in the bag.

'Okay, girls,' he said. 'Here's the plan. In a moment, we're going to pull up and kill the engine. I'm going to open the back doors and take you inside. You don't scream. You don't shout. You don't try to struggle. Follow these simple rules and I won't have to hurt you. Once we're inside, we can talk about how you can both get out of this nice and safely. Got it?'

There was a brief movement from both girls.

'I'll take that as a yes.'

WHITE VAN
MELROSE ESTATE

As the van slowed to a halt and the ratchet of the handbrake sounded out, Amy checked her restraints. She pulled her wrists slowly, feeling how much slack she had.

A voice behind her said, 'Don't even bother. Those cable ties will cut through your skin before you can break them.'

Amy bit her lip, furious at her own stupidity. Now that she'd felt how much slack there was, she was sure she could get the ties off, but not quickly, and certainly not while she was being watched.

The engine turned off.

Outside, Amy heard a car pass. A moment later, another. The driver of the van got out and she heard him call from outside, 'I'll open up when the coast's clear.'

This confirmed Amy's suspicion that they were in a built-up area. That meant people could be passing, and that meant potential witnesses.

She pushed herself close to Mia and kept her whisper as quiet as she could manage.

'Mia? Click your teeth if you can hear me.'

Click.

'Okay, listen. When we get out of this van – the moment we're both out – scream and split up. You run to the right. I'll run left. Even if you only make a few feet, do everything you can to make a scene. Scream, struggle, kick. Anything to catch attention.'

'Hey!' She felt a kick to her side from man in the back of the van. She immediately tensed, convinced she'd been caught out.

'Move over,' he said. 'When I get out, I'm going to pull you towards me, feet first, so you can stand up. Then I'll lead you in. You'll walk quickly and quietly. Now, sit up.'

Amy felt his large, powerful hands pull her up to a sitting position. As soon as she was upright, she felt him forcing something else on her head. The way he tugged at it, it felt like a baseball cap.

'Keep this on.'

The back doors of the van opened and the driver's voice – lacking the gruff, threatening tones of the other – said, 'All clear.'

The van moved as the stronger man shuffled his way out. Then hands gripped Amy's ankles, pulling her towards the open door.

Amy kept limp. From what the man said about leading her in, she got the feeling they were pretty close to the building. If they were, then their window of opportunity was tiny. As soon as they were both out and walking, she was going to go crazy. But she had to time it just right.

She was pulled forward until her feet touched the road and she was sitting on the ledge at the back of the van.

'Stay right there,' growled the man. 'Right. You next.'

His elbow bumped Amy's side as he pushed past, reaching for Mia.

Amy tried to remain calm. Not long now, but she had to make sure . . .

Mia screamed!

It was too early, *far* too early. Mia was still inside the van – out of sight. Amy's idea had been to cause a scene and drag things out long enough to draw the attention of passers-by.

Mia mustn't have realised. The van rocked and shook as she twisted and kicked and kept on screaming.

The man pushed past Amy, back into the van. 'Shut your mouth. Right now!'

There was a clear thump, but Mia made all the more noise.

Amy had to carry on regardless. While he was inside the van, she took the chance to run.

She yelled like a girl possessed, hands tied, running blind, not knowing if she was headed straight for a wall or a ditch.

From behind, she heard one of her captors call, 'Grab her,' and she could hear one of them running after her.

And then right in front, a horn sounded, followed by the sound of a car shoot past. The shock was enough to stop her in her tracks, just for a second, but it was enough for her captor to catch up.

'You're not going anywhere,' said the voice. It was

the driver, and he didn't sound anywhere near as confident as the other. Amy locked onto the sound of his voice, turned and kicked out. She felt contact and heard him cry out.

In the background, Mia's screams abruptly ceased.

Running footsteps, then heavy, strong arms clamped around her, picking her up, carrying her. Seconds later she was back inside the van, her side sore from the impact, her arms bruised with the pressure of the man's hands.

He clambered in after her. 'Shut the doors!'

Amy's heart was racing. Had the driver of the car seen her? Was he calling for help? Had anyone else seen them, heard them?

And why was Mia suddenly so quiet?

She tried to shuffle next to her like before. 'Mia?'

'SHUT UP!' yelled the man.

But Amy was close enough. She could hear Mia's sobs and breathed a sigh of relief. She had thought for a second, one horrible, terrifying second . . .

Next to her, Mia whispered, 'I'm sorry. I'm so sorry.'

The man was ranting. 'You stupid, stupid *bitch!*'

Amy said nothing at first, listening to Mia's repeated apologies.

'It's okay, Mia,' she said at last. 'We had to try something.'

The driver yelled back from the cab, 'Oh, great. Brilliant! What now?'

'My place,' came the reply. 'It's our only option.'

'You going to tell Carla what we've done?'

'For now, I just want to make sure she's in.' There was a pause and Amy heard the click of a mobile. A little quieter, he said, 'We should have done this from the start.'

The heat from her own breath was slowly suffocating Amy. There was a filthy stench of damp or mildew or something coming from the canvas bag on her head or perhaps the interior of the van. There was another smell, chemical or paint or something, possibly coming from the van itself; it was impossible to tell. Either way, the mix was rancid. Amy felt sick and claustrophobic and struggled to contain her growing panic: if she really was sick, she'd choke on her own vomit and if breathing got any more difficult, she could suffocate. She wanted this rank, choking thing off her face, off her head. She could feel herself losing the battle, desperate to scream out, demand they take it off her, that they let her breathe.

But screaming would make things worse. The hood would remain, but the air would be hotter. She would be one step closer to really losing it, and she couldn't allow that to happen.

She closed her eyes tight and bit down firmly on her bottom lip.

One . . . two . . . three . . .

Seconds passed. She thought of where they should be. She pictured herself with Mia walking through the shopping centre, thinking about last week when they had wandered without a care. They'd bought ice creams covered in so much sherbet, it had died their tongues bright blue. They caught a massive fit of giggles, enough that people were looking . . . especially when Mia tried to take a drink of Coke, laughed again, gagged and coughed so hard that Coke dribble out of her nose – just in time for Dan the Man to appear on the scene . . .

Suddenly, the driver hit the brakes and Amy was yanked back to reality. With hardly a pause, the van reversed, turning sharply as it did so.

The driver's door opened. Amy heard a woman – Carla? – asking about the van, asking why they'd brought a stolen car here.

The man in the back pushed forward and yelled, 'Stand by the back doors. Don't you dare let them get past you.'

'What? Don't let who past?'

As the rear doors unlatched, she heard a growl close and loud. 'Don't even think of trying anything. Got it?'

He shuffled out, then Amy felt rough hands grab her ankles. The man yanked her out of the van and held her firmly by the shoulder. Then she heard a yelp from Mia, and a scrape as she was dragged out too.

The woman was furious. 'What's going on? What are you doing, Micky? Wha—'

Slap!

'Don't use my name.'

'Too late now,' said the other one, the driver.

There was no space for running this time. The hand never left her shoulder as she was frogmarched forward with the clear instruction: 'Inside.'

The slap didn't seem to have an effect on the woman, there wasn't even a shake in her voice as she demanded, 'Just tell me what's going on here. Does Maurice know we've turned into kidnappers for the day?'

'Maurice is gone,' said the driver.

Amy tried to make sense of the names. Carla was the woman. Micky was the strong one, the one who'd grabbed her off the street – Carla's boyfriend? – and this "Maurice" was out of the picture, which meant the only one Amy didn't know was the driver. She kept going over the names, burning them into her memory. Once again, she thought of her dad; if she was going to get through this, she needed to take in everything around her.

As the man next to her spoke, she repeated his name: *Micky*.

'He's only gone and taken the money, hasn't he? He's done a runner with the lot.'

The slap might not have put a shake in the woman's voice, but this news certainly did.

'Oh, Jesus.' She sounded almost winded. 'He sent a text. This morning.'

The driver asked, 'Maurice?'

'Andy Galloway.' There was panic in her voice. 'He was getting no reply from Maurice. I just assumed you'd all passed-out from the booze he brought.'

'All part of his plan,' said Micky. 'While we were asleep, he took the money and ran.'

'So we don't have the money? None of it?'

'You're getting the picture.'

'Hang on,' said the driver. 'What did Galloway want?'

44

'He wanted confirmation that everything was on target, wanted to know we had the money.'

'Well I hope you stalled him.' Micky's voice.

'What for? As far as I knew, everything was fine and dandy. We were home free. We were good to go.'

It was Micky's turn to mutter, 'Jesus.'

Next to her, Amy could hear Mia sobbing.

'So we have two girls standing in our lounge with their hands tied and bags on their heads because . . . ?'

'We need to get that money,' said Micky. 'Except when I came up with a way of getting it, I had the mad idea we still had two days to get it. Tell me. Please, tell me that part hasn't changed.'

'I . . . I don't know.'

There was a clatter of something being picked up, then a series of beeps – a mobile phone's keypad. 'What exactly did you put in your message?' There was a slight pause – he was reading the text. Finally, there was a crash, as if he'd hurled the phone across the room.

'Oh, well done,' he yelled. 'I mean, really. Well done!'

A little quieter, Carla said, 'So what do we do, Micky?'

'I told you not to call me that.'

The aggression in his voice was at a new level. Mia was still sobbing, and Amy was fighting like mad not to fall apart herself.

He grunted something – not even a word, then he said, 'Let's get these two out of the way first. We'll put them through there. Search them first.'

'What am I looking for?' asked the driver. 'Some kind of weapon?' His voice was close. He was coming over.

'A mobile phone, stupid. Just do what you're told, will you? Don't try thinking. It doesn't suit you.'

Beside her, Mia whispered, 'I dropped mine.'

But Amy still had hers, and she couldn't stomach the idea of someone searching her. As she tried to speak up, her voice cracked, 'My bag. Zip pocket on the side.'

Amy heard a rustle, followed by Micky saying, 'Good. You help us out like that, Amy, and we'll get on fine.'

It was the first time he'd used her name and it chilled her to the bone.

She felt the phone pushed into her hand. 'Unlock it.'

'You'll need to take the bag off my head.'

There was a loud slap, and next to her, Mia cried out.

Micky repeated, 'Unlock it.'

He'd known that Amy didn't need to see the screen to unlock the phone. She slid her thumb across the screen, then moved it down, left and diagonally right. The phone responded with a slight buzz.

'I still don't see why we need the two of them.' The driver once more.

'Insurance,' said Micky. He took back the phone without thanks. 'We need her mother to pay up, don't we? So we use her friend as an example of what we're going to do to her. Hey! Amy. Does this thing do video?'

It did, but Amy wasn't going to help in any other way. She kept it simple. 'Don't know.'

'Well, it's got a camera. A photo will do just as well for now. Right. Give me a hand getting them in the dining room. I don't want them hearing anything else.'

WOODSIDE HOUSE
BROOKFIELD

Janice May did her Saturday shopping in the morning, preferring to be away before Amy got to the shopping centre. When they'd bumped into each other before, there had been something embarrassing on both sides. Amy's friends would be perfectly polite and friendly, and Amy herself was just as bright and chatty, but there was something there that didn't exist at home: an unspoken tension that put a divide between them. No matter how welcoming, how open the girls were, Janice felt like she was standing on the other side of a fence. It made sense. She was a parent; they were kids. The divide was there for a reason. So long as Amy was happy, she was okay with it.

When the mobile on the kitchen table rang, nothing sparked alarm on any level. The name on the display: AMY, didn't do anything other than make Janice smile. If Amy was phoning already, it meant she needed to buy something over her budget. Janice put the phone to her ear, preparing herself for some rehearsed story that would eventually build up to the big question.

'Mrs May?'

In that moment, everything changed.

The sound of the voice at the other end shattered any illusion that this was some kind of stupid joke and sparked a confusion of questions: Who was this? Where was Amy? Why didn't she have her phone? What had happened?

The male voice, deep, rough, commanding, repeated her name. Janice May could only reply, 'Who is this?'

She didn't get an answer. Instead she got a list of demands, demands that left her numb. The call was short and clear, leaving her standing, staring at her kitchen, with those demands echoing around her.

'Don't call the police.'

'You will give us twenty thousand pounds.'

'To make our position clear, we will send you a photo showing your daughter and her friend. In that first photo, you will see her friend's legs. If you don't call back to arrange payment, you will receive a second photo. Her friend's legs will be broken. If you hold us up any longer, you will receive a third photograph, showing your daughter's legs broken. You do not want to receive a fourth.'

Janice folded onto the nearest stool, stunned. Then she looked back at the mobile phone as the promised photo buzzed through.

Don't call the police.

She didn't need to.

She had another number to call.

Amy sat on a chair, the bag still in place on her head, hands still bound with a cable tie. Her feet were also bound, by some kind of plastic tape, wound round and round. Whatever it was, it was effective.

The same had been done to Mia. They were ordered to keep quiet, otherwise things would get unpleasant. There was a pause, then the shutter sound from Amy's mobile as a photograph was taken. A moment later, the door closed and they were left in silence.

From the other side of the room, Amy heard Mia whisper, 'Amy? Are you there?'

But Amy didn't reply. Instead, she listened. There was something going on next door. She could hear the one called Micky making demands on her phone. She'd heard enough to guess he was talking to her mother. She couldn't imagine what would be going through her head. At first it would probably be disbelief, thoughts that it was all some kind of practical joke.

Mia sniffed and said, 'Amy. I know you're there. I can hear you breathing.'

Amy broke her silence in a low whisper. 'Do you think they can see us?'

Mia's voice, slightly higher, 'How am I supposed to know that?'

'You can listen. Hang on. I think my hands are free.'

'What?'

Amy was lying, but she had good reason. After a pause, she said, 'Sorry, Mia. Just testing. If anyone was in here, they'd have been right over. Keep your ears peeled. If you hear anything, or anyone coming, give a cough. Okay?'

'Why?'

'Shhh.'

Amy began to move her wrists against the plastic of the cable tie. Tensing her muscles had given her valuable millimetres of space, and by pushing her palms and wrists tight together, she managed to make that small amount of slack just a touch looser.

Slowly, carefully, she began to slide her hands together, to move and pull and gently coax her right hand through the gap. It was very tight, and quite painful, and grew increasingly more painful until she reached a point where she could feel that she was over the worst, when the plastic loop slipped a touch quicker over her skin. With a final twist and a pull, her hand came free.

She couldn't help a small gasp of victory.

'Amy?'

'Keep quiet.' With her right hand free, she reached up and whipped the hood from her head.

Micky snapped the phone shut. 'Job done.'

Stubbs nodded. 'It sounded good to me. Short. Clear. To the point.'

'So long as she follows the rules and doesn't do anything stupid.'

'Like what?' demanded Carla, and looked from one man to the other like they were both completely insane. 'Like call the police?'

'She won't,' said Micky with confidence.

Carla grabbed at her hair and yelled at the two of them. 'Will someone tell me this isn't happening, that this is a wind-up. I can't believe you've just phoned that girl's mother with a ransom demand.'

'Calm down,' said Stubbs, holding his hands up.

Carla smacked them away. 'Calm down?' She turned her attention to Micky. 'Kidnap? Ransom demands? Have you lost your mind? Is there any sense of reality – *at all* – in that lump of meat you call a brain?'

Micky stretched his neck, bending his head to the left and right, then he looked Carla square in the eye. 'I'm thinking perfectly reasonably, Carla. We are up to our necks here, and thanks to your text message, we have zero time to come up with the goods. Alternatively, you can pick up your mobile, call Andy Galloway and tell him to hold back on the deal.'

'We should tell him to forget the whole damn thing! If Maurice is gone, who's going to sell the guns?'

Micky remained cool. 'He had buyers lined up.'

'Yes,' she snapped. 'That's what he *told* us. But if that's really the case, if it was all so straightforward, then why did he do a runner? Who's to say it wasn't all one big con? Who's to say he didn't come up with the whole story just to get us working like dogs, collecting all that money just so he could do a runner with it?'

Carla stepped away, driving her fingers through her hair to stop them from shaking. Stubbs just stood there, waiting for a reply from Micky.

'Well first of all,' said Micky, 'he would never have involved the likes of Andy Galloway. Maurice isn't stupid. Plus, I overheard him talking to one of the buyers.' Carla tried to interrupt, but Micky shouted her down. '*And* I overheard him talking to that buyer when he thought he was the only one in the flat. The deal was real, Carla. I'm sure about it. Now he's either got nervous of working at such a big scale, or the sight of all of that money drove him nuts. I don't know, but right now. Right NOW, we have a situation. And we don't have much of a choice of how we cope with it. We've put the order in, so we continue with the deal, and we buy the guns.'

Carla snapped, 'Oh, right, and what? Try to sell them ourselves?'

'That's the next problem. We sort the first now. In ten minutes I'm going next door, and I'm going to do what needs to be done to make that girl's mother pay up.'

Carla gave a sardonic laugh. 'You're going to break that girl's legs? With what? Are you going to nip out and buy a sledgehammer?'

'Have you seen the size of that chopping block in the kitchen?' He gave Carla a quick wink. 'No need for a sledgehammer.'

'This is insane.' She turned on Stubbs. 'Say something!'

But Stubbs remained silent.

Micky nodded. Their agreement was made.

But Carla battled on. 'You actually think her mother has that kind of money just lying about the house. You think she's going to pay up just because you made a threat?'

'No. I think she's going to pay up when she get's that second photo. And time is against us.' He turned to Stubbs. 'You know what we need. Go get it.'

Carla watched in disbelief as Stubbs stood up. 'Micky, stop! You can't. This . . . this is real life, Micky, not some TV movie.'

'I know what I'm doing.' He took a step towards Carla. 'We need to convince that girl's mother we're serious. And when we do, she'll pay up. She'll pay up because her daughter is worth *double* what we're asking, and I happen to know first-hand that she is more than capable of covering the cost, so don't take me for an idiot, Carla. Like I said, I know what I'm doing.'

From the corner of the room, beneath the Blu-ray player, the mobile that had been cast aside vibrated briefly against the laminate flooring before it rang.

They all looked at the phone as if in shock that the thing was still working.

Carla picked it up and read the screen.

Her eyes met Micky's as she said, 'It's him.'

Micky snatched it from her grip and answered. 'Mr Galloway?'

There was a moment of quiet from Micky Carlisle as he listened to the caller.

'Yes,' he responded. 'We have the money, but we don't—'

In the silence that filled the room, the others could hear the response: a strong Glaswegian accent hammering out through the tiny mobile's speaker. 'But me no buts, my man. Tell me it straight. Are we still on?'

Micky paused, glanced at the others.

'Yeah. Sure.'

'Good. Now open the front door.'

Micky frowned, 'Sorry?'

Carla and Stubbs were looking in horror at the shadows visible in the frosted glass of the front door.

'Oh Jesus,' whispered Stubbs.

The phone went dead, just as the handle on the front door turned.

Finally free of the heavy fabric, Amy sucked in air. She was dripping with sweat, her hair was stuck to her brow and cheeks, but she gave it little thought. As soon as the sack was off her head, she got straight to work on the tape around her ankles, stretching it with her hands, kicking and twisting her feet, and finally lifting her legs up, bending forward with ease, and snapping through the tape with her teeth.

'Amy?' Mia's voice was quiet. 'What's going on?'

Amy got up and whipped the hood from Mia's head.

'We're getting out of here. That's what.'

Mia's eyes were wide. 'How did you . . . ?'

'Shh! Don't talk until we're out.'

Amy yanked open the curtains, flooding the room with light and revealing two large French doors.

She bent down and began untying Mia's feet, once again using her teeth for speed. As she did this, she took in the rest of the room to get a feel for the kind of place they were trapped in. As far as she could see they were in a fairly ordinary, quite modern, house. This room, presumably the dining room, appeared to be used to store junk. There was an overflowing ironing basket dumped underneath a small, square dining table, which was pushed against the wall with books and magazines piled on top. It certainly didn't look like the room was for dining.

Nothing about this room said "kidnappers". What it did say was they were disorganised. They hadn't planned the kidnap. They hadn't even thought ahead to clear the room, or to realise that the right hand of the French doors – possibly to save it being lost – still had the key in place.

Amy had her way out.

Outside the doors, the garden was small with a six foot, panelled fence. She could see other houses, but they were much further away than the length of another back garden, which meant that over that fence was either a road or a path. More good news.

Without the hood she could hear the voices on the other side of the door. It sounded like there was some kind of argument going on. Thankfully, the door was solid, with no glass or anything to allow their captors to see that the girls were free.

As Amy tried to bite her way through the thick plastic of Mia's cable tie, she heard a mobile phone ring, cutting next door's conversation to silence.

'What's going on, Amy? Who are these people?'

'I've no idea, but I'm not sticking around to find out. Jesus, this stuff is tough.' She had used her canines to bite pockmarks into the plastic, weakening it, then pulled and stretched and bit down again. With a final tug, the plastic snapped apart.

Mia let out a brief, 'Ow.'

Amy held up a hand, then turned her attention to the door, listening carefully. There was something going on in there. The front door had opened. It sounded like more people were coming in.

This was not good. Not good at all. Not only had they captured her and Mia and tied them up, but they had invited others along.

'We need to move,' she said, stepping back. 'You ready to run?'

Mia rubbed her wrists and glanced about the room. 'Too right. Let's go.'

But as she stood up, the backs of her knees hit the chair, knocking it backwards. She twisted, fast, and tried to grab it.

FRONT ROOM
ASHDALE CRESCENT

The man stepped through the unlocked front door and into the room. He was mid to late forties, lean, with a stern face, greying hair and a hint of stubble. He was flanked on either side by huge, black-suited bodyguards.

'More of a courtesy call than anything else.' He tucked his phone into his back pocket. 'I believe you have some money for me.'

Carla could hardly get her words out. 'I . . . I thought we had arranged a date. Two days' time, wasn't it?'

Galloway strode into the centre of the room. 'If you've got the money now, why wait?' He was scanning the walls, the ceiling. 'Besides, I always like to check out a drop personally before the goods turn up. Just to make sure everything is as it should be. Part of my occupation is avoiding risks, avoiding those people who'd like to see me out of business. Also, I like to get a feel for the people I work with, to look into their eyes before we go any further. Then I count the money, check it's all there. In my business, it isn't just the police you have to be wary of.' He gave a short dry laugh. 'Never trust a criminal, eh? But once I'm satisfied, I'll give you a call back and arrange a location for the goods to be delivered.' He turned his attention to Stubbs to add, 'I don't like to get my own hands too dirty.' He winked. 'You know what I mean?'

Behind the light-hearted words, the air of threat was heavy.

Micky cleared his throat, tried to look relaxed, scratched the back of his head and said, 'Thing is, Andy . . .'

Galloway rolled his eyes and one of the bodyguards growled, 'It's Mr Galloway to you.'

It was enough to shake Micky up. He wiped the side of his nose with a hand and dropped his eyes. 'The thing is, Mr Galloway. We've had a slight situation with the money. One of our team's done a runner.'

'You wait until I turn up to tell me this? Are you telling me that you want to cancel our deal?'

'No!'

Galloway's eyebrows raised a small degree and Micky immediately lowered his voice. 'I just mean that we've got things in order. By this evening, we'll have it. I guarantee.'

'You know where this other person is, do you?'

'Not exactly, but we'll have the money.'

Galloway sighed and shook his head. 'Maybe I didn't make myself clear when the arrangements were made. Not only did you assure me you could *get* the money, but five minutes ago on the phone, when you thought I was a little further away, you told me you *had* the money, and that our deal was still on. I can't help the feeling I'm being messed about here.' He moved away, as if weighing things up, then he turned back, his eyes narrow.

Before he spoke, there was a sudden, loud 'clank' from the dining room: the sound of a chair falling against a radiator.

In a flash, the bodyguards had guns in their hands. Galloway took his own gun out, deliberately, slowly, and aimed it at Micky's face.

'If this is a set-up, boy, you die first.'

As soon as the chair hit the radiator, Amy was at the French doors. She twisted the key and yanked the handle.

At the same time, the dining room door burst open. A man the size of an ogre, dressed in a black suit, was aiming a gun right at her.

'Stand still, miss,' he commanded. He pointed to Mia. 'You too. Stay right where you are.'

Amy knew she didn't have a chance. Even without a gun trained on her, she'd still have the fence to contend with. If she was alone, she might have taken the risk. If she was alone, she might even have made it. But she wasn't.

Reluctantly, she gave up and turned away from the open door.

By then, there was a second man in the room. He was dressed like the first and just as big. He kept his gun steady on Amy while the first man shut and locked the French doors.

The men said nothing more, just held their positions until a third walked into the room. This one was slim with short grey hair and stubble. Physically, he was nothing compared to the other two, but the way they stood firm, silent, disciplined, waiting for this third man's reaction, made Amy feel he was much more dangerous.

'I want to know exactly what is going on here.' His accent had a dirty, broad Scots brogue, and everything about him, his grim expression, even his suit jacket, worn casually over a plain black T-shirt confirmed that he was the man running the show.

Amy's mind raced. She knew enough to realise that the situation they were in had somehow escalated. The men who had kidnapped her came across as vicious, violent, but disorganised. This man was different. It wasn't just his two armed bodyguards, it was his manner, the way he had walked in, the casual way he held his own gun. He carried an air of competent professionalism that terrified Amy May.

Once inside the dining room, the grey-haired man turned and flicked his head to usher the others to follow. The bodyguards shuffled further into the room to make space, the one next to Amy nudging her closer to the wall. As the others – the two men and the woman – stepped into the dining room, the man with grey hair pointed his handgun at one in particular. 'You'd better start explaining.'

'Like I told you . . .' Amy immediately recognised the voice of Micky. His height, build, even his ugly, twisted mouth, matched his tone perfectly. '. . .we got ripped off. Maurice did a runner with the money.'

The Scottish man demanded, 'And?'

'We thought we had time. You know.'

'Don't beat about the bush with me. Just tell me straight. Is this what it looks like? Kidnap and extortion?' He looked at the girls. 'How old are these two?'

It was Mia who muttered, 'Fifteen.'

Micky's voice raised slightly. 'Wait a second, now. These aren't just a couple of random girls. They're gymnasts. Olympic standard, and their parents . . .' He pointed to Amy. 'Well, hers at least, is not short of a few bob. I'm telling you, by six this evening we'll have your money. The deal can still go ahead, and we can all go our separate ways.'

Behind Micky, Amy noticed how the other two – the driver and the woman, presumably Carla – were hanging by the door. The driver wasn't nearly as tall as Micky. He was moving backwards very slowly, motioning to Carla with his head.

The man with the grey hair didn't even appear to glance, but his words were stern. 'You move one more step towards that front door and it'll be the last thing you ever do, my friend.' He fixed his eyes on Micky and he continued his questioning. 'So, you thought you could deal with this situation, get the money and welcome me with open arms?'

He turned away, and without any more warning, he took aim and fired.

There was a clear, deafening shot and in the main room the man who had just taken a warning not to move fell to the floor. Carla screamed, her hands slapping to her face in an attempt to stifle her own cries.

Micky held up his hands, panic plastered across his face. 'Woah, Andy man, cool it. We can sort this out.'

'It's Mr *Galloway*,' growled one of the guards.

'Sorry. I'm sorry! Mr Galloway.' He waved his hands, fingers splayed like they might stop a bullet. 'Look, I'm serious. These girls. They're special. We'll have the money in a few hours.'

Galloway lowered the gun. 'How did you do it?'

'What?'

In the background, Carla was whimpering. The driver was lying still, face down into the carpet. Amy could make out a pool of spreading blood around his body. She glanced at Mia. Mia was standing perfectly still, staring with wide eyes. There was no way she could see the body from where she was, but she was staring all the same.

Galloway's voice had calmed, but it still had a dangerous edge to it. 'I asked you a question. How did you do it? How did you make the ransom demand? Did you use the phone?'

'I'm not that stupid.' Despite the fact that his colleague was lying dead just a few metres away, Micky's tone was controlled once more. 'I used *her* mobile. The girl's. I called her home direct. That way, it's traceable to the daughter. No link to us.'

'Your idea?'

Micky folded his arms, apparently quite proud, and nodded. 'That's right.'

Galloway nodded. 'When? How long? Give me minutes.'

Micky shrugged. 'Ten. Fifteen? Not long.'

'So right now, the police will have been contacted . . .'

'I told her not to contact the police.'

'Kidnappers usually do. But parents know this is too big for them, panic takes over and they contact the police regardless. And the very first thing the police do is to trace the kidnappers' call.'

Micky held up Amy's mobile and glared back, defiant. 'And it goes straight back to her own address.'

'The call is traced to the *phone*, my friend. To wherever you made the call *from*. Understand?' He sighed. 'No. I don't suppose you do, and I'm not going to waste my time talking about receiving masts and triangulation. Just be assured that it's only a matter of time before you get another knock on that front door.'

Galloway walked towards Mia, looking her over, touching a hand to her shoulder to turn her. Mia turned without argument.

'When that knock comes,' he continued, turning his attention – briefly – to Amy, 'you will be taken into custody. You will be questioned, at length. And sooner or later you will mention my name.' He looked directly at Micky Carlisle. 'And as I'm here, in front of you, you can even give an eyewitness description. Can you see where I'm going with this?'

Another whimper from Carla spurred Micky into stepping backwards, his valour finally crumbling.

Galloway continued. 'But you expect me to hang around for another four hours?'

Casually, he checked his gun.

Micky ran for the front door.

Galloway turned to face Amy and smiled. Behind him, one of the bodyguards stepped into the front room. Micky was at the front door, pulling in frustration, having realised a little too late that one of the bodyguards had locked it and removed the key. He turned, with his back against the door, hands in the air. 'No, don't. Plea—'

His cry was cut short by two successive gunshots. As he fell, Carla screamed, no longer trying to control her cries. It didn't really matter. Another gunshot, this one aimed at her, punched Carla across the room, where she fell with a crumpled thump.

Galloway kept his eyes on Amy.

Inside she was burning up. Inside she was firing off multiple scenarios of how this could turn out, replaying stories from her father, recalling everything she could in the wild hope there was a way out, *any* possible way out.

'And now there is only you,' said Galloway. 'Two young girls.' His face was stone. 'You've been brought into something through no fault of your own.' He began to raise the handgun. Amy took a breath, seeing the chamber of the pistol come into focus right in front of her face.

'For that,' said Galloway, 'I am deeply sorry.'

Amy had no doubt what was coming next. It wasn't just the barrel of the gun or the tone of that man's voice. It was something that welled up deep from within, call it instinct, fear, panic – whatever it was, it screamed out that she wasn't going to get out of this alive.

Her eyes were locked onto the gun. A semi-automatic pistol. Like the one her dad had shown her.

'A simple move.' He had placed an unloaded gun into her hands. 'But unlike self defence, this relies more on confidence than skill.'

But right now, she didn't have the confidence. Right now, she wanted her dad to burst through the door and take over. She could feel her stomach turn to jelly, hear the whimper from her own throat and knew, without any doubt, that if she didn't seize that confidence, she and Mia would –

Her right hand flashed upwards, across her body – palm turned outwards – and grabbed the muzzle of the gun. As soon as her palm touched the hot metal, she snapped a tight grip, turning it back towards Galloway rather than away, then slammed the butt of the gun with her left hand to release it from his fingers.

The movement took a second. Fast. Accurate. She could barely believe her own success, that Galloway didn't have time to respond, nor the strength to stop the gun being snatched.

And now it was hers, transferred seamlessly to her right hand as she stepped back. She held a perfect aim at the Galloway's forehead, supporting her right hand at the wrist, her index finger already pulling a pound of pressure on the trigger.

Sudden movement on either side told Amy that the bodyguards had their own guns trained on her, but she didn't flinch, didn't blink and didn't release the pressure on the trigger.

The reaction from Galloway was more surprise than panic. He raised his hands in surrender, a wry smile on his face. 'Easy, young lady. Easy. If you didn't have the safety catch on, you might even be dangerous.'

To her right, there was a slight snigger from one of the bodyguards.

Amy didn't falter and didn't drop her aim as she spoke. 'I know how to use a gun. There's a bullet in the chamber, it's cocked, unlocked and very ready to fire.'

Galloway's smile was frozen for a moment, then it actually broadened.

'My, my,' he said. 'What *have* we got here? How can a fifteen-year-old girl disarm a man like a pro?' His eyes narrowed. 'Who taught you something like that?'

Amy didn't answer. Internally, she was going over a

list of instructions, one of which was not to be pulled into conversation. She had one single goal: escape. She was not going to be diverted.

Galloway, with his hands still in the air, slowly turned to look into the main room. He actually stepped aside, as if to give Amy a better view of the man by the front door, lying face down, perfectly still, dark blood soaking into the carpet.

'It takes a lot of guts to snatch a gun like that.' Galloway turned back to face her. 'And it takes guts to point a gun at a man's face. But it takes something else to pull the trigger, to see your victim's forehead take the impact, the back of his head explode in brains and blood as he falls, and to live with the fact that you ended his life.'

His smile dropped and he lowered his hands.

'It takes a certain kind of person. I'll give you ten out of ten for effort, little girl, but I can see it in your eyes; you aren't going to fire that gun.'

Despite her best efforts to keep her hand still, Amy could feel the tip of the gun begin to shake. She kept the pressure on the trigger, but it was like her finger was locked. Even if she wanted to, she couldn't put another gram of pressure on that thing.

Galloway's hands were at his sides. 'You're not a killer, miss.' And after a pause, he added, 'Pity.'

WOODSIDE HOUSE
BROOKFIELD

Amy's mother was left to wait, locked in a perpetual rollercoaster ride of panic and fear with nothing to do and nowhere to go. She boiled the kettle three consecutive times before actually making a cup of tea, and even then she let it go cold. All she could do was keep going over what her husband had told her on the phone.

'Just sit tight,' he'd said. 'I'll get someone over there right away.'

'What about you? Can't you come?'

There was a pause. His voice was low. 'You know I can't.'

'This is our daughter!'

He didn't answer. All he said was, 'I'll get someone there for you. I promise.'

When she heard a car pull up outside, she shot to the window. One man, one woman stepped out, both in suits. They scanned the house and surrounding area, the man holding a phone to his ear and talking the whole time, only ending the call when they approached the house.

Janice was at the door before they had a chance to reach for the bell.

'Have you heard anything?' She said, not trying to hold back the strain in her voice.

'Mrs May,' the woman said, holding out a hand and following up with a stream of automated apologies and regret for this 'terrible situation'.

Janice wasn't interested. She wanted answers. 'So what do you plan to do about it?'

The man stepped forward, effectively directing Janice back into her own hose. His voice calm with authority. 'There are a range of strategies in every hostage situation, Mrs May. Some require time, patience and negotiation.'

Janice actually laughed. 'So, what? You're going to wait until they call, have a chat?'

The woman took over, explaining in a quiet, but firm voice, '*Some* require patience and negotiation, Mrs May. In this situation, however, from what we have gathered so far, we think the kidnappers may well be amateurs. Low-grade criminals out for a quick profit.'

'And what makes you so sure?'

'Several things. The relatively low ransom.'

'It might be low to you . . .'

'With respect, Mrs May, big-time criminals wouldn't take this level of risk for a few thousand pounds.

'And that's good, is it?'

'Yes it is. If they're inexperienced, they won't have a back-up plan, or an exit strategy. They'll make mistakes.'

'Mistakes?'

'Yes, Mrs May. Such as using your daughter's mobile phone. We tracked it to an address just a few miles away, and in a short while we will have a substantial team of armed officers surrounding that house.'

Janet straightened. 'I want to be there.'

The man came over. 'I'm afraid that isn't possible, Mrs May.'

'I'm just expected to sit here and wait? I don't think so. I know how these things work and I know you'll be setting up a remote viewing. I'd like to have a link in here.'

'Mrs May, with respect –'

'Don't "with respect" me! If you won't take me to the house, then I want a laptop set up on that table with a live feed. I am not going to sit and wait for reports when I know for a fact that a link will be set up as soon as your team get there.'

The man sighed, and Janet was ready for his counter argument, but the woman spoke up before he had a chance. 'If that's what you'd like, Mrs May, then I'm sure we can arrange it.'

Mia couldn't scream, she couldn't speak, could barely get her breath. She didn't know if Amy was dead or alive. All she knew was that Amy was on the floor, lying just as still as the three adults who had been shot, after one of the bodyguards swiped the back of her head with the butt of his gun.

Galloway stepped forward, looked down and simply said, 'Interesting,' before bending to retrieve his gun.

'Change of plan,' said Galloway, as he straightened back up. 'We'll take the girls with us.'

The other bodyguard placed a hand on Mia's shoulder. Mia felt herself wince on the inside, but her body remained frozen.

A single piercing bleep rang out. Galloway pulled out a mobile and checked the screen.

'Looks like our friends in the Force are on the move,' he said. There was no panic in his voice, it was just a matter of fact statement. 'Unusual, but I'm not going to hang around to ask why.' He pointed to Amy. 'Pick her up. The other one can walk. Let's get out of here.'

He turned away and went back into the front room.

The first bodyguard leaned down and picked Amy up, casually lifting her body over his shoulder. The other nudged Mia. 'Go.'

In the front room, Mia could hear sounds coming from the kitchen – a loud, wrenching noise, then a bang followed by a loud hiss. Galloway came back into the front room, pulled a zippo lighter from his pocket, flicked open the lid with a thumb and struck the flint-wheel. As the flame took hold, he placed the lighter squarely on the table and walked towards the door.

Mia's eyes fixed on the flame.

'Keep moving, miss,' said the bodyguard behind her. She felt a nudge, but came to a halt regardless, confused as to why he would do that, and why there was still a loud hiss coming from the kitchen.

She snapped her gaze away from the lighter, blinking against the spot of glare to see the crumpled bodies of the three adults, blood seeping into the carpet around them. The driver was face down, the other, bigger man, was on his back, mouth open in a silent scream. But the woman, she was on her side. And when Mia looked into her wide-open eyes, she didn't see the lifeless glaze of death. She saw her blink, she saw a hint of movement on her lips, and she felt her looking back with genuine, living terror.

A hand grabbed her arm and she was pushed the rest of the way out of the house.

There was a car parked on the drive. Bigger, better – even blacker than the car Amy's mum drove.

As they approached, the driver got out and opened the rear passenger doors and spoke to Galloway.

'If this is a set-up, you owe me fifty quid.'

Galloway took a quick look down the street and walked to the passenger side of the car. 'A wee bit more complicated than that, Mack. Get us out of here in good time, and I'll entertain you with every detail.'

Mia was pushed inside the car. At the same time, the other door was opened and the limp body of Amy was dumped on the back seat, held in place with the click of a seatbelt. The bodyguards climbed in next and sat opposite.

Short, clear police messages came out through the car's stereo.

'You've certainly got someone's back up,' said the driver. He pulled out into the road. 'We've got about six local units heading this way with orders to seal the roads, plus three armed units speeding down the A19. ETA for the armed boys, about eight minutes. The others are coming from the city centre, so unless we're really unlucky, we should slip out in plenty of time.'

'Well done,' said Galloway. 'You've earned your keep for another day, eh?'

The car moved quickly, above the speed limit, but not recklessly.

The driver spoke up as they hit the roundabout and turned right onto the main road. 'And . . . we're out.'

Mia looked across at Amy. She was still slumped, and from this angle, with the movement of the car, it was impossible to work out if she was even breathing.

As she watched her friend, Mia finally understood the meaning behind the lighter and the hiss from kitchen. Galloway had turned the gas on – or from the noise he'd made, he'd ripped the whole pipe from the wall. Either way, the result was clear. When the gas met the flame . . . boom!

But why hadn't he left Amy there, like they'd left the woman?

For that matter, why hadn't he knocked Mia out too, and left them both for dead?

Inside the house, Carla lay on her side.

She kept reminding herself that by some miracle, she was still alive. She had tried calling out to Micky, to Stubbs, but couldn't get her voice. She was feeling increasingly weak, increasingly cold and dizzy. If she moved, the pain in her stomach spiked so much that it felt like she'd been cut in two.

Outside, she'd heard sirens. She had seen the flashing red and blue lights reflecting on the walls, the ceiling. Right now, she could hear shouts and orders. The house phone began to ring.

She could also hear the hiss of the gas in the kitchen.

And she could see the flame of the zippo lighter on the table.

It was only a matter of time.

WOODSIDE HOUSE
BROOKFIELD

Janice May sat in silence as the female agent set up the laptop. Beside her, the male agent was explaining the operation. 'We'll try to establish communication first, get them talking, make sure the girls are okay. Then we'll make it clear that they have only one way out of this.'

The image of the live feed appeared and Janice was slightly taken aback.

Such an ordinary house.

'I'm afraid we don't have sound,' said the female agent. 'Give me a moment.' She fiddled with the computer's settings. 'Ah. There we go.'

Janice could hear chatter orders coming through the small laptop speakers, officers nearby replying, one of them running in front of the camera to take a position closer to the house.

She said nothing. She just watched, hardly able to believe that her own daughter, and her daughter's best friend, were inside that house.

'I'm afraid this could take some time,' said the male agent.

But then the screen flashed white, and the speakers gave off pure white noise, unable to process the sound as the front door blew out, and the windows – frames, glass and half of the wall – exploded with a fireball that filled the screen.

Janice clapped her hands to her mouth. Images of officers ducking down against the searing heat, retreating, shouting. Screams from neighbours.

And beside her, the female agent. 'Oh my god.'

Janice May couldn't speak, couldn't blink.

That was it. Over. Because there was no way, no way at all, that anyone could survive that.

LIMOUSINE
M1, HEADING SOUTH

Pain. Dizziness. A low drone of an engine, the feeling of movement.

She opened her eyes carefully, just a fraction, to see what was going on. She could see the suited legs of the bodyguards, their shoes so big she couldn't guess the size. She moved ever so slightly to get a better glimpse of her surroundings.

The car was massive. It must be some kind of limousine, with enough space back here so that the black leather seats were facing each other. To her left, she could see Mia's trainers.

Up front, she heard the voice of Galloway. 'We're in for a long drive, young lady, we might as well get acquainted. Your kidnappers said you were Olympic standard. That true?'

Mia replied, 'Amy is.'

'So what are you, her sidekick?'

'Training partner.'

'Right, so she's a local celeb, is she? This Amy . . . ?'

'May,' said Mia.

Amy winced at that, wishing she could tell Mia to keep her mouth shut.

Galloway nodded. He had something in his hand. From the way he was fiddling, Amy guessed it was a smart phone. This was confirmed when he nodded and said, 'So she is.' He smiled. 'The internet's a wonderful thing, isn't? I've got a full story right here.' There was a pause as he scanned the article. 'It mentions a training partner, but not your name.'

'Mia.'

'Mia? Nope, not a thing. Still, must be nice to be working for someone heading for Olympic gold, eh?'

Amy had heard enough. She had to intervene, so she moaned then blinked her eyes, lifting her head slightly.

'Amy?' The relief in Mia's voice was backed with concern. 'Are you okay?'

Amy just groaned. She was still trying to assess the situation. The bodyguards had noticed her, but said nothing.

Galloway twisted a little more in his seat. 'Amy. Back with us, I see. Your friend was just filling us in on a few things.' He briefly motioned his phone. 'But for now, make the most of the rest. You've both had one hell of a morning, so I'm happy to avoid blindfolds or sedative – unless, of course, you make it necessary. Know what I mean? We've got a long drive ahead of us, and I'd like it to be as relaxed as possible.'

Amy still acted sleepy, but up ahead, she noticed the road sign. It was blue, which meant they were on a motorway. The side windows were tinted, but not so dark that she couldn't make out the junction number as they shot past.

Galloway gave a small chuckle. 'Take it all in, young lady. Doesn't matter one way or the other. All I ask is that you keep things relaxed and quiet. If you do anything silly, my boys will have to react. I hope you both understand.'

Amy glanced up at Galloway's humourless face then immediately averted her eyes, focussing instead on the cabinet between the bodyguards and the way the light reflected on the polished walnut finish. Everything about this car reeked of money, the tinted windows, the space, even the smell of leather.

Slowly, she adjusted herself to sit upright. She noticed Mia's concern and simply nodded to say she was all right.

From up front, she could hear voices: quiet, tinny messages. It took a moment to realise she was listening to the police radio channel.

'Might as well turn that off,' said Galloway. He reached out and killed the signal. 'Show's over.'

The station was replaced with AC/DC singing 'Highway to Hell'.

Amy didn't react. It was nothing more than a bad coincidence, and she had more to think about than reading meanings into chance songs on music stations.

For one, why was Galloway not bothered about her checking the road signs? Was their destination a ditch at the side of the road? Why bother? Why take the risk of putting her, with Mia, in the car in the first place, only to take more risk in finding a secluded spot to kill them. It didn't make any sense.

Beside her, Mia whispered, 'They blew up the house.' Her face was streaked with tears. There was a distinct shake in her voice too.

Amy reached over and gave Mia's hand a squeeze, then she spoke up, directing her question at Galloway. 'So what are *you* planning to do with us? Is this a kidnap? Another one?' She gave a short laugh. 'Two in one day? What are we, the unluckiest girls in the world?'

'Not exactly.'

'No? What does that mean? If you're going to kill us, why didn't you do it back there, when you murdered the others?'

Galloway turned and gave her a frown like she was a baby. 'I'm afraid you've got me all wrong.' Then he smiled, but his grin was devoid of warmth and his words were chilling. 'If you play your cards right, darling, you could well be my new best friend.'

Quietly, Amy said, 'You've got to be kidding.'

'I never kid. Those men kidnapped you because you had something they need. And now, you've got something that I need. At least, I'd like to think you have. Be grateful for small mercies, young lady. It's the reason you're still alive. Let's leave it there, shall we?'

Then he turned away, reclined his chair and leaned back. 'Wake me up when we get there, Mack. I'm going to have a snooze.'

After two hours, the car finally took an exit and cut

through farmland on quiet country roads. Mia finally spoke up. Her voice had lost its panic. If anything, she sounded angry. '*Where* are you taking us?'

The bodyguards didn't react.

'Tell me!'

Beside her, Amy said nothing. Waiting. Watching.

There was a grunt from the front passenger seat. Galloway turned briefly then yawned. 'Found your voice, have you?'

'I just want to know what's going on.'

'Well, your timing is spot on, little girl. We're just about to arrive at my place in the country.'

The car took a left into a long, narrow road. As far as Amy had seen, there had been no signs to either indicate a left turn or where the road would take them. The road was dim due to the trees on either side, which arched above.

Eventually, Amy could see two large metal gates up ahead with a name, curled into the metalwork: *West Hall Manor*. As they slowed their approach, the gates opened. There was no operator, but Amy noticed an intercom panel fitted into a recess in the right gatepost. As they passed through, she caught sight of a tall perimeter fence, hidden on the inside by a hedge. Somewhere, unseen dogs barked. A moment later, the driveway opened out and she got a view of the house itself.

She heard Mia whisper, 'Oh my god,' and, frankly, Amy had to agree.

This wasn't just a place in the country. It was the sort of mansion you find in a TV period drama. It was massive, with three floors and more windows poking out of the steep, high roof.

As they drew closer, the gardens that had at first appeared so impressive began to look a bit rough and overgrown. The hanging baskets fixed to the exterior walls were empty, leaving it to the imagination to picture how this place was meant to look. Amy could only make the assumption that Galloway didn't care about aesthetics. But if that was the case, why had he bought such a place?

In front of the house was a circular drop-off area where several other vehicles were parked. The driver took the curve slowly, parked and pulled on the handbrake.

'Home sweet home,' said Galloway.

DRIVEWAY
WEST HALL MANOR

Stepping out of the car, Galloway gave orders to the bodyguards. 'Take the girls upstairs. Put them in a guest room – separate rooms, actually. I need to talk to our Michelle, decide how best to handle this.'

He walked through the main hall and into the library, a large, airy room with huge bay windows and plenty of natural light. There were stacked shelves on the walls packed with everything from finance to tax to fine art. There were also several computers.

Sitting at one of them was the slender figure of a woman in her late thirties. Her dark brown hair was a mass of curls so wild that Galloway had to get close to see the images she was currently scrolling through.

'Well, well. While the cat's away, eh?'

The woman minimised the screen, but didn't turn. 'You could always knock.'

'Why? Are you doing something you shouldn't?'

'What I do in my time is my business.'

Galloway had seen enough to know exactly what she was up to. 'Feeling nostalgic, are you?' He shook his head. 'I don't know. I never understand these social networking sites. Why people put all of that personal information up for the whole world to see is a mystery to me. I do hope you're being careful.'

'I'm always careful. Don't worry. False accounts and proxy-skipping – there's no trace.'

'You just sneak into their accounts and spend the morning browsing old photos, eh? Oh, believe me, I'm not complaining. In fact, it's what makes you the perfect person for the little job I have in mind.'

Michelle turned to face him, her expression impassive. 'Job?'

'Aye.' Galloway sat against the desk. 'We had a bit of a situation this morning. The whole thing ended up a total and utter shambles. Unfortunately, it involved a couple of teenage girls who witnessed a few things they shouldn't. My business instinct was to take them out with the others, but what can I say? My good side won me over.'

'There's no such thing.'

Galloway tipped his head and considered for a second. 'Well, let's say one of these girls could get me out of a rather sticky situation. I'm just making up my mind how to approach it. But time is of the essence, and I get the feeling she'll be a reluctant employee.'

'That sounds rather ominous. What about the other?'

'She doesn't tick the same boxes, but who knows? She could have potential. For now, though, she's got a more important role. I'd like to offer her friend a choice, but one that she can't refuse. You know what I mean?'

'I really hope I don't.'

'Let me spell it out then. First of all, contact our friends in the city. Tell Marge to expect a guest.'

'What?' Michelle looked suspicious. 'How old did you say these girls are? Eighteen? Sixteen . . . ?'

Galloway held up a hand. 'I didn't.' He wasn't going to get into this now. 'Tell you what, I'll call Marge myself. I want her to know exactly what to expect – and what's at stake. In the meantime, I'd like you to find out as much as you can about the other girl. I Googled her in the car. She was kidnapped because she's a gymnast, and a good one. We're talking top ten, here. But I've a feeling there's a little bit more to her than that. So I want you to do a real search on her. Considering her day so far, she's bound to be on some news channel or other. Find out what they're saying. See if they give any background info.' He tapped the top of the monitor. 'Then you can hack into *her* Facebook account rather than your old school chums. Check out her friends, family. Especially her family. Like I said, I think there's a little more to this girl than gymnastics.'

BEDROOM
WEST HALL MANOR

Amy wasn't sure how long she'd been left in that room. Certainly more than an hour. She'd spent some time looking out of a window, down on to a courtyard that she assumed was in the centre of the house. She could see the windows of rooms on the far side, curtains open, but nothing going on inside. And just like the garden below, the small pond, borders and bushes – it was all very nice, but it gave away nothing about the location of the house or why she was here. And nothing about its owner.

Her own room was tastefully decorated, although old fashioned. The bed was a double, but no four poster. The carpet was deep pile and cream. The door was solid, and the lock substantial. It was an old fashioned ward lock – the kind that required a large, chunky key. Amy checked the drawers, just in case. She didn't only look inside, but pulled them right out, checked behind, underneath. She pulled out the wardrobe, checked the back, the top and behind. She looked under every shelf, even the back where something could fall and be wedged, or deliberately hidden. She did the same with the bed, the window sill, radiator. She checked every inch of that room, but there was nothing. Certainly no key, but nothing that could be used as a pick. No forgotten Allen key or hair grip, and the coat hangers in the wardrobe were plastic.

In frustration, Amy had thrown herself on the bed and now lay there, facing the ceiling.

She thought about the events of the day, from being in the gym, talking to a reporter, to finding herself in the back of the van. She could recall the faces of her captors clearly, as well as the sound of the gun, scenes of them falling to the floor, images of them lying dead. And then Amy was running out through the French doors where she vaulted the fence with ease, calling back to Mia, 'Run, Mia. Now.'

She was on the opposite side of that fence, looking back, calling to Mia. But Mia looked terrified. She was crying. She was crouching low as the man pointed the gun at the top of her head.

And then a loud, piercing scream.

Amy woke. She hadn't realised she'd fallen asleep, and while it was a relief that the image of Mia was just a dream, she had no doubt that the scream was real.

It came again: higher, louder. Mia. She sounded like she was terrified, or fighting. A second later, she heard her cry out, 'Amy!'

Amy shot onto her feet and hammered on the door. 'Mia? Mia! What's going on?'

But there was nothing else. She heard distant footsteps, and muffled voices, but no more screams. Amy thumped the door again, shouting for Mia, calling her name for some kind of response.

Minutes passed. No more sounds. No more screams. No more footsteps. Eventually she withdrew and walked back to the bed. Twenty or more minutes later, there was a click from the lock and the door opened. Amy sat up to see a tall woman in black jeans, loose white top and wild, dark hair.

'Hello, Amy.'

Amy said nothing, picking up on the athletic build of the woman at the door, trying to assess her age. She failed, but her guess was that the woman was way older than she looked.

'My name's Michelle. I work for Mr Galloway.'

'Really? So where's your gun?'

Michelle took a step into the room. 'I don't have a gun. I wouldn't even know how to fire one. Would you?'

The question was loaded: a full magazine. Amy refused to be drawn. 'Where's Mia? I heard a scream earlier.'

'Mia is . . . she's elsewhere. Mr Galloway feels it's important to keep you apart for the time being.'

'Where *is* she?'

'I'm sorry, Amy. I can't tell you that.'

'Oh really? Well how about you go back out the door, turn the lock and leave me here until you can find someone who can tell me where she is.'

Michelle nodded, as if this all sounded perfectly reasonable. 'Actually, I came to tell you that Mr Galloway would like to see you. If anyone can explain things, he's the one.'

'Fine. Send him in.'

The woman gave a slight shake of her head. 'You don't really think it's going to work like that, do you? Come on, I can see you're a clever girl, so how about you get up and come and find some of those answers you want.'

As Michelle turned back towards the door, Amy considered staying put, refusing to move. But what would she gain? She stepped forward, ignoring Michelle's pathetic attempt at a sympathetic smile, as she ushered her out of the room.

The corridor was spotless, with bedroom doors on the right. The walls were broken up with paintings and, on the left, windows revealed the gardens below and rolling landscape beyond.

As they walked, Michelle spoke quietly. 'You must have made quite an impression. Mr Galloway is very particular about the guests he brings to the house.'

'I'm not a guest.'

The woman didn't react. She continued to walk until the corridor opened out at a spacious stairway. A heavy, baroque banister curved down either side of the stairs to the foyer below. Michelle placed a hand upon it, paused and said, 'Mr Galloway can be a bit hard at times, but that goes hand in hand with business. He does have a gentler side. It might be hard to believe, but he does.'

'And you're telling me because . . . ?'

'Because his bad side can be *very* bad.' She took a deep breath, as if searching for the right words. 'Treat him with respect, he'll return that respect. So, for your own good, lose the attitude and don't antagonise him.'

LIMOUSINE
COUNTRY ROADS

Despite her protests, Mia was escorted downstairs and back into the car. Struggling was useless. The bodyguard who came for her had said she could walk, or she could be carried, but either way, she was going with him. She preferred the first option.

Back on the road, she felt unbearably vulnerable without Amy. She tried to convince herself this was stupid. Amy might be tough, but she wasn't that tough. Even so, it would be comforting to know that she could reach out to feel the warmth of a friend's hand. Instead, she felt lost, alone and very afraid.

The dynamic of the car had changed too. Without that boss bloke, whatever his name was, the driver had turned up the music and Mr Bodyguard was busy playing some mind-numbing game on his iPhone.

'Where are we going?' asked Mia.

This was the second time she'd asked since they'd left the house. The first time she'd just been ignored and she expected the same reaction now, but to her surprise, the bodyguard said, 'Your new home.'

'I've already got a home. Where are you taking me?'

The bodyguard laughed and called forward to the driver, 'Should we tell her she's going to Hollywood?'

At this, the driver laughed. 'Ouch. Mind you, some people would pay good money to see her as the star.'

There was something sinister in the bodyguard's laugh and it knocked the wind out of Mia. A little too quietly, she asked, 'What?'

'Just enjoy the ride, little lady,' said the bodyguard.

Sick of these jokes, she regained her voice and screamed, '*Where* are we going? What the hell are you two talking about?'

The bodyguard just looked at her, one eyebrow raised. Still smiling, he shrugged. 'Depending on your point of view, it could the beginning of a beautiful new career.'

'Tell me!'

'Cool yourself down, girl,' the bodyguard's tone was deep and soft, but there was a hint of malice. 'It's still a long ride, and you're gonna need all the energy you've got when we reach our port of call. So lie back, listen to the music and relax.'

Mia opened her mouth to say something else but the bodyguard raised a finger to silence her. 'Just remember one thing. Those bozos who kidnapped you, who tried to rip off the boss? They were threatening to kill you. Think of that for a minute. You could be lying there dead right now, all burnt up with the rest of them. But you're not, you're here, with us. Face facts, little girl: Mr Galloway just saved your life.'

Mia looked away. She kept her eyes fixed on the world

outside, biting down hard to stop her jaw trembling, subtly squeezing her side to keep the pains in her stomach at bay. In front of her, the bodyguard grunted something inaudible, self satisfied, and returned to his game.

Mia gave him a brief glance. Was he right? Had his boss really saved her life? To what end? Why would someone who had murdered three other people save Mia and Amy? Where was this car really going?

And wherever it was, why wasn't Amy going there too?

MAIN LOUNGE
WEST HALL MANOR

The lounge had two main sitting areas. To the right there were several two-seater black leather sofas, chairs, coffee tables, an enormous widescreen TV and a fireplace large enough to burn a whole tree. But the fire was not burning, the TV was off and the chairs and sofas were empty. In the centre of the opposite wall, double doors opened into a spacious conservatory that looked over the gardens beyond.

In the left hand side of the room were round tables, chairs, as well as a fully functional bar complete with bar stools, beer pumps and barman. There was even a dartboard to one side. Amy took it all in before focusing on the men at the bar.

Galloway was sitting on a stool, engaged in conversation with the barman. To his right sat the bodyguard who had ushered Amy from the car.

'Mr Galloway,' said Michelle, softly.

Galloway turned. 'Ah, Amy. Please, come and join me. Thanks, Michelle. Go find yourself something to do while we have a chat.'

He waved a hand briefly towards the bar. 'A drink? A soft drink, obviously. I don't want my barman here breaking any laws.'

The barman smiled politely; the bodyguard guffawed like it was the funniest joke ever.

'We've got fresh fruit juice,' Galloway briefly lifted his own bottle, 'or diet coke, lemonade, tea, coffee. Richard does a fantastic hot chocolate too, with whipped cream, marshmallows –'

'Water,' said Amy.

'Water? No problem. Mineral water? Sparkling water? Water with a hint of fruit – quite nice that.'

'Just tap water.' Amy kept her guard up, her mind tuned to a story her dad had told her. It was in response to a question about the line of small round scars on his arm. Her dad had explained, 'Cigarette burns. Repeated over and over while they asked me the same silly questions.'

Amy had been horrified. 'Did you give in?'

He merely raised an eyebrow. 'If I'd talked, do you think I would have collected so many scars? By the end it became a competition, a battle of wills, to see how many marks I could knock up before my interrogator gave up.'

As he pulled down his sleeve, Amy had said, 'I don't think I could ever put up with that amount of pain.'

Her father shrugged. 'When someone tries to use force, you know where you stand. It's just a question of holding out. It's the ones who try to befriend you that you really need to worry about. The ones who play it nice, who play mind games. Before you know where you are, you've told them your mission, your inside leg measurements and what you want for Christmas.'

Galloway slapped a hand gently on the bar, breaking Amy's thoughts.

'Richard, a glass of your finest tap water.'

'Certainly, sir.' The barman picked up ice with a pair of tongs. 'Would miss care for ice and lemon?'

Amy didn't meet his eyes. 'Just water.'

'So,' said Galloway, turning to give her his full attention. 'You've got yourself into a right pickle, and through no fault of your own. You were kidnapped because they thought someone had the money to pay up, not because you've got a particular skill.'

Amy said nothing, even when the glass was placed in front of her.

Galloway continued. 'The situation at the house was . . . unfortunate, but unavoidable. I'm sure there are many in my line of work who would have put bullets in everyone. But to me, it was clear that you and your friend were reluctant participants, and completely ignorant of the bigger picture. Thing is, now we have another situation. You and your friend have got a whole load of information that would be of substantial use to our boys in blue. I'm sorry, Amy, but I can't let that happen.'

'Where is Mia?'

'Mia is fine, but it's better for now that we keep you two apart. Call it insurance, just until we understand each other. Right now, I want to talk about you. I mean, what you did back there in the house: snatching a gun like a soldier – wow! A move like that takes skill, as well as guts. So I'm saying to myself, where does a girl like you learn something like that?' He opened his hands. 'Well, it doesn't take a rocket scientist to work that one out, does it? Your father was in the army, I believe.'

Amy immediately dropped her gaze down at her glass.

'Oh, come on, Amy. You're a local celeb. In the papers and everything. It's no wonder those idiots targeted you. The first thing I did when we got here was to get Michelle to see what else she could find out about you. It makes for impressive reading.' He indicated several sheets of A4 paper lying by his right hand. 'From the look of it, you've more medals and trophies than you can probably fit on your shelves. Let's see now, "Daughter of Janice May, previously Janice Mitchell..." She trained as an accountant, nothing particularly outstanding there. I found this interesting though. Your father began a military career with the British Army on leaving school.' He nodded like he approved. 'I'm guessing he passed on some of his hand-to-hand combat skills, eh? Which explains your move with the gun. Nice.' He looked back at the papers. 'Our Michelle is pretty good when it comes to hunting down information, but she couldn't find much more about him. It's like he joined the army and disappeared.' He pushed the papers aside. 'Regiment, was he?'

This time, Amy kept her face rigid, refusing to be led.

'Sorry.' Galloway held up his hands. 'Slip of the tongue. I meant to say, *what* regiment was he? Silly me.'

But Amy knew it was no mistake. She only hoped she really had maintained her mask. When people talked of being in a regiment, they were talking of which leg of the army you were in. When people talked of being in *The* Regiment, it meant something else entirely.

'I'm a serviceman myself,' continued Galloway. 'I missed the Falklands by a whisper and spent four years in Northern Ireland.'

Ex-army? Then it really was no slip of the tongue when Galloway had asked about The Regiment.

He gave a dramatic shrug and stretched. 'It didn't take me long to realise it wasn't for me, though. Standing on a street, an ordinary street with houses and cars and washing lines, holding a gun and telling people what to do while children yell abuse or throw stones at you. On the positive side, it was where I made a lot of business contacts, people who wanted to fight for themselves.'

'And where you started trading arms.' Amy looked directly at Galloway. She didn't attempt to mask her disgust.

But Galloway just grinned. 'Oh, there I go, talking about me, me, me.' He took another sip from the bottle. 'All I'm saying, Amy, is that you caught my attention back in that house. I have a bit of a dilemma. I don't want to keep you here against your will, but I can't let you go talking to the police. What we need is a way of establishing mutual trust. If we achieve that, then we can go our separate ways, no harm done to either party.'

Amy paused, unsure. 'And how do we do that?'

'Well, that's something I'm busy working on.' He sniffed and sat up straight. 'And while I'm doing that, I'd like you to take things easy.'

Amy's mouth twisted. 'Is this your way of saying I'm going to get locked back in my room?'

'On the contrary. I'd like you to wander. Take a good look around the house. There's a games room you can use, a cinema room – we've got all the movie channels and a massive DVD library. Or go outside, around the gardens, the tennis courts. Spend some time getting a feel for the place, for what's on offer.'

'On offer?'

Galloway nodded. 'That's right. Get a taste of how I live, how *you* can live if you want to.' He stood up, preparing to leave. 'Enjoy the comforts, Amy May. Because in a short while, things are going to turn rather unpleasant.'

LIMOUSINE
INNER CITY

Mia's car journey felt endless. Realistically, it wasn't anywhere near as long as their earlier drive, but without Amy by her side, it seemed to go on forever.

When they pulled off the motorway for the second time that day, there was no country road to follow. Instead they were driving through some built-up inner city.

They came off the main streets, away from the shops and office blocks, wove their way through residential areas and eventually pulled up against the kerb. The driver killed the engine and the body guard opened the door, leaning forward to say, 'Time to get out.'

Mia stepped onto the pavement of an ugly, run-down row of terraced houses. There was litter on the ground, choking the gutter. The remains of a burnt-out wheelie bin lay abandoned on the opposite side of the road where several of the houses had their windows and doors boarded up with metal sheets.

'Of course, when we said Hollywood,' said the driver, 'there was a touch of exaggeration in there.'

The bodyguard found this amusing. 'Pretty good movies in my book.' He winked at Mia. 'We get them at a cheap rate.'

Mia felt her skin crawl under his gaze and had to turn away. At the same moment, the front door of the nearest house opened and a heavy-set woman, mid fifties with battle-worn features and a cigarette in her hand, stepped out. Without any formalities, she growled, 'Take her along the end. Jade is waiting for her,' and as almost an afterthought, she snapped, 'And you can move that car!'

The driver smiled at the bodyguard, and in a low voice said, 'She's a gem, our Marge.' He indicated the direction for Mia to follow and added, 'And that's her on a good day. Face of a pitbull, body of a bus and a heart of ice.'

From her step, Marge yelled out, 'Be quick about it!'

The driver ushered Mia again. 'Come on, love. Best learn to do as she says.'

Everything in Mia's body screamed out at her to run. She remembered Amy's advice when they were about to get out of that van. She had told her to run and scream like mad, and Mia had a good idea that she'd give exactly the same advice here.

She stopped walking. Her feet were fixed to the spot and her stomach tightened to a knot. Suddenly Mia knew, without question, that going through any of the doors in this terrace was going to be the end of her.

Her legs went weak and she felt herself slump.

'Woah,' said the driver. 'That's not going to help.'

But she didn't care. If she collapsed, maybe they'd put her back in the car, take her back. Maybe . . .

The bodyguard's grip tightened on her shoulder and yanked her up. 'No time for games, love.'

Footsteps behind, then the hulking figure of the old woman was there, right in front of her.

'Tired, is it?' She grabbed Mia by the hair, tight, vicious, and pulled her head up. 'Are you a clever girl? Eh?' Her breath was rank: black coffee and nicotine had stained her teeth, but there was an underlying stench of gum disease, tooth decay or something equally rancid. Before Mia could answer, the woman tightened her grip. 'Then you best learn the house rules, and learn them fast. Number one: do as you're *told*!'

She gave Mia's head a shove, snatched her hand away and growled at the men, 'Get her inside. Now!'

Galloway left Amy sitting at the bar and made his way to the library, confident he'd find Michelle there.

He gave the open door a hard knock with the back of his fist and Michelle, sitting at the same computer as before, turned.

'Is that better?' he asked. 'Didn't want to creep up on you unannounced.'

'Very funny.'

'You found any more details about our guest?'

'Only what I gave you earlier.'

'And her friend?'

'Nothing of any great interest. She's Amy's training partner, and best friend. They've been close for years.'

Galloway eyes almost sparkled as he replied, 'That's exactly the information I want to hear. I want to play on this best friend thing. It's one hell of a crowbar to help our Amy make up her mind.'

Michelle didn't smile. 'When you say "crowbar" I take it you don't want me to be particularly subtle about this.'

'No, no no, Michelle, that's precisely what I *do* want you to do. Subtlety all the way, and no details about where her friend is or what's in store for the poor wee lass. I want to give Amy that news myself, gauge her reaction. She seems a decent enough girl, the kind who wouldn't let her worst enemy face what we've got lined up for Mia, but she's got to have something positive to weigh it up against. I want you to make the good side so attractive that it won't really be a choice at all. Gain her trust.'

'And how do you expect me to do that?'

'Do what you do best, Michelle. Lie. Let her know which side her bread is buttered, eh? And on the subject of food. Alice should be firing up the kitchens around now, give Amy a menu, let her know she can order anything she likes. I want her to see the better side of this place, you know what I mean? And while you do that, I've got the rather tricky prospect of informing Jake Salinger of recent events.'

An electronic beeper sounded in the main hallway. Galloway looked to the door. 'Uncanny! That may well be him now, so make yourself scarce. Besides, it's a beautiful summer evening out there.' Galloway paused at the door, looking back into the library with a nostalgic smile. 'Those pastel shades of tranquillity bring a long day to its end, eh? Really sets the house off. Part of the reason I took up the lease on the old place. Anyway . . .'

A figure appeared at the doorway: stocky, muscular, with short cropped hair and a touch of stubble on his chin. His eyes were on Galloway, but for the tiniest moment, they flicked to Michelle.

'I got a message you want to talk.' His voice was gravel, annoyed, with a slight East End accent.

Galloway's expression changed. 'My office, if you don't mind.'

Without checking to see if Salinger was following, Galloway walked along a corridor and unlocked the door to his office.

The room was busy, but not disorganised. Bookcases were full, broken up only by the odd ornament or photo. Other photos, of varying sizes were fixed to the walls, and in the centre of the room, a large desk was piled high with papers and folders.

Salinger sidled inside. 'So what's the problem?' There was a small grin on his lips. 'Am I in for a caning here or something?'

'Close the door.'

'Sounds serious.'

'Close the door!'

Salinger closed the door. When he turned, Galloway was sitting at his desk, arms resting on the marked, wooden surface.

'I hear you've had a bit of a day,' said Salinger, slumping into one of the chairs on this side of the desk.

'That would be putting it mildly,' said Galloway. His eyes were locked on this larger, stronger man, daring him to come back with another joke. Finally, he continued, 'I was in a particularly foul mood before I even arrived at that house, and that's not the way I like to operate. Bad moods can cause bad judgements, my friend. And this one nearly caused me to miss a diamond opportunity. I'm talking one in a million.'

Jake didn't joke. His tone reflected the anger in his face. 'Is there a point to all of this?'

'The point,' said Galloway, 'is the cause of my foul mood. The fact that last night, while you were trying to complete your second job, someone else was in that building.'

'We dealt with it. Whoever it was, they heard us coming, dropped the painting and legged it.' He shrugged. 'My guess? Just some small-time burglar taking a chance.'

'Oh, right. It's just a coincidence? A small-time burglar? Don't be so naïve.'

'So what are you suggesting?'

'I'm suggesting there's no such thing as coincidence. This was pre-arranged. Not only did they target the same painting, they specifically set out to go after it on the same night as your team. This isn't about stealing a painting. Someone is going out of their way to embarrass me, and that is only possible if they had been forewarned.'

Salinger's face was stone. 'Choose your words carefully, Mr Galloway. *My* team, as you put it, are made up from people *you* employ. Your driver, your bodyguards. If you think there's a weak link in the chain then it's in your organisation. Not mine.'

Galloway held his gaze for a moment. 'That might not be a million miles away from what I'm thinking. Call it paranoia, Jake, call it self-preservation, but I'm far too cynical to believe in chance meetings of burglars in the night, especially when it involves something that is being stolen to order.'

Salinger sighed. 'I got you the painting, isn't that the main thing?'

Galloway slammed a hand on the desk and shot to his feet. 'No, Jake! It is *not* the main thing. If there is some toerag out there trying to steal from under me, trying to make me look incompetent, trying to take me for a fool!' Spittle flew from his mouth. 'It adds to the risk of the job by several thousand per cent. Whoever it was didn't only drop the painting, potentially damaging the thing, but he did a runner.'

Salinger didn't rise to Galloway's fury. 'The only reason he got away was because we thought he was a security guard. We had a choice: go after this guy, or get the painting, get out, and get it safely back to your good self. Or would you rather we filled the air with bullets at the first sign of trouble?'

Galloway sat back down. 'I pride myself on my word, Jake. If I tell a buyer I can get something he wants, I don't want to have to call him back and say "sorry, pal. Someone beat me to it". But right now, there's someone out there trying to do just that.'

'Then you should be more careful who knows which paintings you're going after.'

'You may have hit the nail right on the head, there.' Galloway paused. He reached into a drawer and took out an envelope. He removed several printed sheets and photographs and sifted through them. While he did this, he said, 'This final piece, have you given it much thought?'

'I haven't spoken to anyone, if that's what you mean.'

'Well, the situation is simple. We've managed to get two of the paintings my buyer ordered, but this is the one that will seal the deal. It's worth more than the other two put together. So I want to keep this particular job as tight as possible. And that includes the team. So, how do you feel about operating alone on this one?'

Salinger gave a single shake of his head. 'Not possible. I'll need at least one person for cover. The security on that painting is high tech. I can't just take it off the wall. I'd also like to be assured that my exit is clear.' He leaned across and tapped one of the photographs. 'This is our problem. That building is eighteen stories, and the painting is kept in the penthouse – the very top floor. To me, that's nothing more than a vertical dead end. I don't care for the chance of being trapped, so – in normal circumstances – I'd like one man on the ground floor to keep watch. But now that there's an added risk, I'd like to make that at least two, fully armed. If this rogue burglar tries the same trick again, I'll have someone on the ground ready to take him out.'

'And if I don't agree?'

'Then you don't get your painting.'

Galloway interlocked his fingers and leaned forward. 'So there's no other way?'

Salinger let out an irritated sigh, a tone of aggression in his voice. 'What do want me to do? Fly in through the window?'

And like a chess-master, seeing the end moves, Galloway's smile formed slowly. 'What if I gave you an accomplice who *could* do that?' He gave a slight head-shrug. 'In a matter of speaking.'

Salinger actually laughed. 'Is this a wind-up?'

Galloway didn't waver. 'No wind-up, Jake. Do you remember that diamond opportunity I mentioned? What would you say if I could give you someone who is probably less than a third of your weight, half your age and twice as fit?'

'I'd say you were either lying, or pulling my leg.'

'I thought you might,' replied Galloway. 'But with things as they are, I'd rather it wasn't you collecting that painting at all.'

Salinger's eyes narrowed. 'Just say what you *do* want, Mr Galloway.'

'Oh, don't worry, I'm not giving you the sack, Jake. Far from it. As it happens, I totally agree with your assessment of the job. This building is a vertical dead end, and the last thing I want is you, one of my best assets, caught by the filth.'

'Or do you mean questioned?'

'Both. So, in this instance, I'd like you to supervise things. From a nice, safe distance.'

'So who *is* going for the painting?'

Galloway paused for effect. 'Someone special. A girl. Well, more than a girl, let's say she's a rather gifted young lady. Athletic, nubile, subtle. She also has the advantage of knowing very little about me and absolutely zero about our buyer.'

Salinger snorted. 'Sounds too good to be true. Is she up for the job?'

'I've a bit of persuading to do on that matter, but that's all in hand. Once we have her on board, however, I have no doubt she'll be able to complete the job successfully.'

'Oh yeah? What makes you so sure?'

Galloway smiled. 'Because you, my friend, you are going to train her.'

Amy stood in the conservatory, looking out at the landscaped gardens at the back of the house. They were impressive, but no better than those at the front. Close by, in the raised beds, she could see a metallic stem of what looked like a fountain spout hidden within the leaves. It was turned off, and the tip showed signs of rust. Whoever owned this place previously must have had these gardens looking stunning. Now, cracks were beginning to show and weeds were pushing their way out between the paving stones of a meandering path.

'Mr Galloway said you are free to wander.'

Amy turned to see Michelle standing just behind her: a shadow in colour, mimicking her posture, pretending to gaze out at the gardens too.

Amy asked her, 'How long have you been standing there?'

Michelle stepped past her and opened the doors. 'It might do us both good to get some air, don't you think?'

Amy stood firm. 'Where is Mia?'

'Let's not start that again, Amy. We both know I'm

not going to tell you. Let's try to keep things light, eh?' She stepped outside, waiting for Amy to follow, but Amy kept her feet rooted to the spot. Finally, Michelle gave a sigh and said, 'If it's any consolation, I found it pretty tough when I first came here. And like you, it wasn't by choice.'

Michelle turned away and began walking.

Still on guard, Amy followed. 'Are you trying to tell me *you* were kidnapped?'

Michelle was a little further along the pathway. She continued walking, but turned a fraction, waiting for Amy to catch up. 'Mr Galloway didn't kidnap you, Amy. He rescued you.'

'I was thrown in a car and driven here. And now that I'm here, I can't get out. Looks like kidnap to me.'

Michelle stopped and pointed a finger to the side of the house. 'If you follow your way around the house you'll see the driveway. The gates are operated by intercom, but there's a keypad override. Two-nine-four-two. That should do the trick.'

'You saying I can just walk out of here? I heard dogs barking when we came in.'

Michelle checked her watch. 'You shouldn't have any problems there. The dogs have a run that goes between the hedge and the fence – all the way around, but blocked in at the gates. They'll bark, and probably let the whole world know you're leaving, but unless you try to climb the fence, they shouldn't cause you any problems. So yes, if you really wanted, you could walk out of here.' Her eyes met Amy's. Amy couldn't help the brief fantasy of taking Michelle at her word, of legging it to the gates, punching in the numbers and running for all she was worth. So if it wasn't the gates keeping her here, then what was it?

The answer to that was simple: Mia.

And from the poorly hidden smile on Michelle's face, she knew it too.

'I worked as a financial adviser,' said Michelle. She started walking once more, moving from the path to the lawn. The grass was spotted with weeds, daisies, clover. Michelle looked up at the clear sky and once again gave Amy the chance to catch up.

'I started doing some work on the side for Mr Galloway,' she said. 'After a while, I began to see things that could do a man like him a lot of damage if I decided to share them outside his circle. But in helping him with his accounts, I had actively chosen to *be* inside that circle with him. At first, I felt uncomfortable, then frightened, trapped.'

She smiled, as if that was enough to explain everything, then she seemed to change track completely. It was like someone had clicked a switch. Even her tone was lighter as she indicated the area ahead. 'Tennis courts. Beyond them, a reasonable golf course if you're that way inclined. Mr Galloway likes to entertain a lot, but we're free to use the facilities if we wish. That includes the gym . . .'

'Gymnasium?'

'I use it as a dance studio. And it's quite a size. It has multi-gym equipment, weights, step platforms, stuff like that. No parallel bars or anything, but we can get those for you if you want. There's also a spa, sauna and small pool.'

'Is that what's kept *you* here? A few goodies to stop you feeling like a prisoner?' Amy shook her head and gave a small laugh. 'My grandad used to keep rats. Real smelly things, even if they had just been cleaned out. But he loved them. You know why? Because they were intelligent. Cleverer than hamsters and mice. So he used to teach them tricks. Not for fun, but because they needed it. A wheel alone won't do, see? Rats need things to play with, puzzles to solve. Otherwise they spend their time trying to escape.'

Michelle's smile dropped. She held Amy's gaze, then she looked out at the tennis courts, back at the house, at the lawns, the surrounding hedge and the countryside beyond.

'What is freedom?' she asked. 'People talk about it all the time, but what is it? What exactly is freedom, Amy May?'

Amy didn't have to think long. 'Being able to choose.'

Michelle put her head to one side, then nodded. 'I agree. Okay then. I guess one day I woke up, and I realised I had more choice here than I ever did back home. I had a decent job, with a fair wage, some prospects. I'd have been okay. And then Mr Galloway began to put the pressure on. He wanted me to leave my old job and work for him full-time. He brought me here, and at times I did think of this house as a prison. But after a while, I managed to put things into perspective. If I had worked for a hundred years in my old job, I would never achieve a life like this. And yet here it is, on a plate. All I had to do was accept the changes in my life and agree to stay.'

Once again, she looked back at the house. 'Mr Galloway isn't a bad man. I think he used to be, but he's saved me from years of struggle in a dead-end job. He's rewarded hard work with respect, with a decent wage.'

'You make him sound like Mr Wonderful.'

Michelle didn't answer.

Amy stood there, watching Michelle, wondering what was really going on behind those eyes, and why they suddenly looked so distant. Finally, she spoke up. 'Yesterday, I saw him murder three people. I thought he was going to kill me too. And then Mia.'

'You're not dead.' Her eyes were cold now. 'And I promise you, Mia isn't either.'

'So where is she? You're the one being all honest here, so where is she? And why weren't we murdered with the others?'

Michelle held Amy's gaze, and for the briefest moment, Amy tensed. But Michelle didn't move. She just spoke, slowly, carefully. 'Mr Galloway is a businessman. He's ruthless to a degree you can't even imagine. When you get to know him or, more importantly, you get to know the people he does business with, then you'll understand . . .' She paused. 'But it all comes down to business. To succeeding at any cost.'

'Are you telling me . . . ?'

'I'm telling you to tread carefully. Mr Galloway

doesn't give this lifestyle away for free. He thinks you've got something he wants, Amy. You need to convince him he's right, because that's your ticket to freedom.' Michelle looked at her, eyes serious, her tone low. 'And it's the only way to free Mia.'

NO. 12
THE TERRACE

As Mia stepped into the hallway of the last house on the terrace, she recoiled at the sweet, sickly scent inside. It was too strong for the pathetic, dying flowers she could see. More like a cheap air freshener, the kind you use to mask bad smells, rather than its pleasant fragrance.

The dying flowers stood in a vase on a desk, pushed up against the wall. There was a telephone on that desk and an open netbook. Two modern items in a hallway that would otherwise look like a relic from the nineteen sixties. From the look of it, the lampshade had neither been changed nor dusted since then. The carpet was worn, and the floral, flock wallpaper was yellowed and peeling where it met the skirting.

There was a man sitting in the chair next to the desk. The cordless phone was tucked between ear and shoulder while he tapped notes on the netbook. Behind him, a woman was watching as Mia shuffled into the hallway.

'Hello, Mia,' the woman said. Her voice wasn't kind,

but not nearly as abrasive as Marge's, younger, too. 'I'm Jade. And you're in room six with Scarlet, second floor. I'll take you up, get you settled, then get you something to eat.'

'I'm not hungry.'

'Fair enough.' There was no edge to her voice, no threat or sarcasm. 'Follow me.'

Mia took a moment to look behind her. The bodyguard was standing at the door. Jade paused at the foot of the stairs. 'Oh, he's not going to stay there, Mia. We've been here long enough to know how to keep our girls secure and safe.'

Mia couldn't believe this was still happening. What was going on? Why had she been brought here? She felt her voice wobble. 'By "safe", do you mean "keep them locked up"?'

Jade continued up the stairs. 'No. Just safe and secure. You'll understand soon enough.'

A bell on the table buzzed. Mia looked back at the door and she saw a flash of red hair just behind the bodyguard.

A voice rang out, 'Excuse me!'

The bodyguard shifted to one side and Mia saw a young woman, possibly twenty years of age, and again, that bright-red hair, cut in a tight, angular bob. As she pushed her way past, she rolled her eyes and said, 'Why thank you – oh, not at all.' Things were made all the more difficult by the carrier bags in her hands, each branded with the logos of familiar high street shops.

Mia just stared. Those bags. Those names. The kind *she* should be carrying through her front door. That's where she should be right now. Home. Safe. Not . . .

'See what I mean?' said Jade. 'Scarlet treats the place more like a hotel than a home.'

Mia snapped herself back. 'Scarlet?'

The girl handed something to the man on the desk then looked up at the sound of her name. 'Someone talking about me?' She was short and slim with delicate tattoos of vines and flowers weaving up her bare arms, over her shoulders and up to her neck. Large eyes shone with humour – natural beauty amplified with make up as loud as her hair, lipstick as bright as her smile.

'Just us,' said Jade and flicked a finger between herself and Mia.

She skipped to the foot of the stairs and followed them up. 'Who's "us"?'

Jade placed a hand on Mia's shoulder. 'This is your new roommate. And from what I've heard, she's had a bit of a rough day.' She gave Mia a subtle, but friendly squeeze. 'I think she could do with some rest.'

Scarlet's room was small and simple. There were two single beds. One was made, but covered in clothes and bags; the other looked like someone had just got out of it.

Mia stood in the doorway as Scarlet fussed about, pulling a brightly coloured top from one of the bags and checking it against herself in the full-length mirror

– a mirror surrounded by photographs of Scarlet and other girls, all waving and posing for candid snaps, taken in pubs and clubs.

'I'll shift my stuff off the bed in a mo. I didn't realise I was going to have company until an hour ago, and I had a few things to grab.' She turned and smiled again, but this time, there was slight edge. 'I never share make-up, so don't ask, and I don't do drugs – other than that, I'm fairly easy going.'

Mia just nodded as this strange red head chucked things here and there. She returned to the mirror to check a second, equally garish top. Mia was surprised that despite the familiar brands, the clothes Scarlet was holding up were so different from the ones Mia would be taking out of the same bags right now. She couldn't imagine showing off anything like that.

'The bathroom's just along the hallway,' said Scarlet. 'The lock's a bit dodgy, so make a lot of noise when you're in there if you don't want surprises. There are washing machines two doors down, but we like to keep our stuff separate from the women down the block. I'll show you which ones we use – or if you're really paranoid, there's a launderette just two streets away.'

Through the haze, Mia heard herself mutter, 'Where am I?'

Scarlet laughed. 'Well, until you come to your senses and realise that working in a bank is a far more respectable way of making money, you're in Little Hollywood.' She bounced on her bed and lay back.

'What?'

'It's just our pet name for it. Helps us hold onto the mad idea that we might be stars some day.' She looked Mia up and down. 'And I've got to say, you've certainly got the body for it. That's probably why you managed to get in, eh? We always get the lookers in here. It's part of the job. So long as you aren't camera shy, it's a better option than being on the game like the rest of the girls in the terrace. I can't think of anything worse than having some overweight local slobbering over you. Ugh.' She winced and shook her head, then her smile returned and she asked, 'Don't mean to pry, babe, but you don't half look borderline.'

'Borderline?' No. *No*! She couldn't possibly mean . . ?

'You know,' she flashed a smile, a knowing nod, a shared joke. *'Borderline*. Movies that go under the tag, "Barely legal".' She wiggled two fingers on each hand for the inverted commas – nail varnish flashing red as it caught the light. Then she waved her hand away like it was nothing to worry about. 'Oh, don't worry. It's the tag I used to play. I've always looked four years younger than my real age . . .' Scarlet's voice faded, and her smile dropped.

But Mia was barely aware. She knew the place was suddenly quiet. She knew that Scarlet was looking at her with concern rather than humour, that she had shuffled forward and sat up, but she couldn't quite allow herself to believe what she was hearing.

Gently, Scarlet's voice broke through her thoughts. 'Are you okay, babe? You don't look too well.'

Mia didn't know where to start, or what to say.

Scarlet gave her a sympathetic look. 'Is there someone out there who didn't like the idea of you coming here?'

Mia began shaking her head, slowly at first. This wasn't true. Couldn't be true. 'Like the idea of . . . ? I don't even know where I am. Are you talking about *porno* movies?'

She looked up to see Scarlet's eyes flick from the door back to her. Mia paused for a second, then turned to see if there was someone behind, but Scarlet leaned forward and put a hand on Mia's knee.

'Mia? Look at me, babe. Look at me.'

When Mia met her eyes, Scarlet said, 'How old are you? I mean, for real?' She shifted to the edge of her bed, knocked the door closed and repeated her question. 'How old are you, babe?'

Somehow, Mia found her words. 'Fifteen.'

Scarlet seemed to deflate. 'Oh, baby. What are you *doing* in a place like this?' She kept her hand on Mia's knee and gave it a slight squeeze. 'You shouldn't be here, love. I didn't realise. I don't even know what they're thinking, but really, *seriously*, you should not be here.'

CONSERVATORY
WEST HALL MANOR

Amy kept looking at the hedge that hid the perimeter fence, the fence that ended in those huge, automatic gates. It was getting on for late afternoon and the sun's heat was waning. It was exactly the sort of Saturday afternoon people dream of. And out there, beyond that fence, in back gardens up and down the country, people would be firing up the barbeque, making the best of the weekend weather, while she stood here, going over Michelle's advice, as well as the code she'd given her.

Two-nine-four-two.

She'd silently repeated it over and over, just in case.

But where was Mia?

What was going on back home? The police would be involved by now, surely. Well, considering there'd been a kidnap, a triple murder and a house blown to bits, the police most certainly *were* involved, but from what Galloway had said in the car, did that mean there was no trace, no way of finding out where she was? The one thing she picked up on, over everything else, was that Andy Galloway wasn't only professional, he was also very thorough and very, very careful.

And he'd seen something in Amy – something he must want very, very badly to risk all this.

Amy found herself walking around the side of the house, looking for the gates.

Two-nine-four-two.

All she had to do was run to the main road, wave and shout to flag down a car . . .

But where was Mia?

The irony, thought Amy, was that she had everything here she could want. Tennis courts, pool, gym . . .

It's not the bars that make a prison.

The thought conjured a flash of memory. The image was of her father, but the voice was her own.

'But you were there against your will.'

Her dad was sitting in the front room, a closed book on his knee and a glass of whisky in his hand – a rarity, and something he only ever sipped. He carefully placed it down on the small table to his right and turned to face his daughter. 'You can spend your life in places against your will, Amy. Just listen to all those people who complain about their jobs. So, yes, I was there against my will, and technically I was imprisoned. But it's not the bars that make it so.' He tapped the side of his head. 'It's what's in here. It's whether or not *you* consider yourself a prisoner. You can feel as much a prisoner in a palace as you can in a cell.'

'They took you to the palace?' Amy knew how stupid

the question was as soon it came from her lips, but she couldn't help it. If her dad so much as hinted at a story, even as a teenager, she was hooked. And so far, this promised to be a belter.

'Thankfully, our captors weren't that close to Saddam,' he said. 'And this happened before the war in Iraq broke out. Had it happened later, then we probably *would* have been taken to the palace, and we'd have been tortured, beaten, humiliated and most likely stuck in front of a camera. But this was during the months leading up to the war. The United States were convinced that Saddam had weapons of mass destruction and they were determined to get him out. So there we were, in Baghdad, collecting as much information about his forces as possible, finding out just how elite his Elite Republican Guard really were.'

'Is that who captured you?'

'It was bad luck that got us caught. To be honest, it looked like they couldn't believe they had us. They knew from our weapons alone that we were British, but it was their leader who realised what we were.'

'Their leader?' asked Amy, her eyes wide. 'You don't mean . . . ?'

Her father smiled and sat back. 'No, not Saddam. The Republican Guard is made up of cells, groups of soldiers under the command of a single leader. It was a bit of a joke really, these idiots had stormed in but we were up and ready to fight. It didn't matter that we were heavily outnumbered. The four of us were back to back in the centre of a room facing sub-machine guns on all sides, and then we hear, in English, a cry of, "Wait!" And then he came forward . . . The biggest Iraqi soldier I ever saw. Six foot four, and as wide as a bear. He had stubble all over his chin, right up his cheeks and a missing tooth as he grinned. He began laughing, but not in a menacing way – he looked like a kid at Christmas.'

'What did he do?'

'He said the words I hated more than any other. He looked me in the eye and said, "Special Air Service." It wasn't a question. He knew we were SAS, and he was over the moon.'

Her dad leaned back and picked up his glass once more, taking the tiniest sip. 'This was bad. This is the sort of thing that could make his career, and every one of us knew it.' He placed the glass back down. 'We had no choice. We surrendered our weapons, we were escorted outside into vans, and we were taken to their base.

'There was some argument when we got there. The leader grabbed one of them by the throat, slammed him against the wall then kicked him unconscious. My Arabic was pretty good, but he was ranting so fast that I could only pick bits out. It didn't take much to decipher the general message though: if anyone wanted to go against his authority, then he'd stamp them down.

'He had a dilemma, see? On one hand, he could turn us over and get himself a medal or a nice pat on the back. But on the other, he'd just found the source of his own personal obsession. The Regiment is renowned, the world over, as the best of the best of the best, and here we were, in his base. We were prisoners, yes, but he saw us as something extra special, and he wanted to treat us that way. So he gave us an offer.'

'An offer?'

Her father nodded. 'He wanted us to train his men.'

Amy pulled back. 'I hope you told him where to go.'

'Why? Do you think if we agreed, we'd be traitors? Helping the enemy out?'

Amy did, but she didn't say so; she just shrugged.

Her dad pointed a finger. 'That's the voice of youth talking. Experience helps you fight those knee-jerk moral reactions. Our primary objective was to get in, get information and get out, right? We weren't at war, not yet, so regardless of how they saw us, from our point of view, *they* were not the enemy. But they could have had us on charges of spying, which would mean imprisonment and torture, and that really would have compromised our mission. So we agreed to his terms. We realised that by helping them, we could learn more about the Republican Guard than anyone back home could. In short, we couldn't believe *our* luck.

'They confiscated our weapons. They wanted them for themselves and trained them on us while we began teaching some of our techniques – fairly simple stuff, hand-to-hand combat, but nothing fantastic, not even the things I've shown you. Remember, if we got out of this, and war was declared, then we could be facing these men in battle for real. As we worked with them, we got an insight into their own military tactics, strategies, and one-to-one capabilities. And this is important, because the key to our escape was right there in those details. We got to *know* our enemy, not just by their methods, but how they talked to each other, the conditions they lived in, even the way they dressed and washed. We took in every detail because we knew at some point it would provide us with the key to our escape.

'The men weren't so different from ourselves. They all had families, loved ones, friends. They were doing a job, just like us. That common ground led to respect, which led to trust, which made their security measures lax, giving us the opportunity to make an escape.' He shrugged. 'Nothing dramatic. Nothing gung-ho. Over the weeks, we stashed knives, nails, bits of pipe. Then one night, during a game of cards, we turned on our guards, took their weapons, knocked them out cold and slipped away. Job done.'

Amy gave a massive, impressed sigh of relief.

Her father smiled and continued. 'It's like I said: It's not the bars that make a prison. And none of us thought of ourselves as prisoners. We were at work, gathering information until the time was right to leave. We used it as an opportunity. And that is what separates a prisoner from a survivor.'

He sniffed. 'Of course, when we got back home –'

'Philip!'

Amy's mother was at the door. 'I *thought* I heard voices down here. And Amy, I thought *you* were in bed.'

Amy stood up. 'I was. I came down for a drink.'

Her mother frowned, shaking her head slightly as her gaze switched from daughter to husband. 'She needs her rest.'

Amy's dad twisted to check the clock. 'It's a Friday night, not even half ten. Other kids her age –'

'Other kids haven't got training in the morning. Go on, Amy, get upstairs while there's still some of the night left.'

Amy clapped a hand on the arm of the chair. 'Night, Dad.' She kissed him on the cheek, then went upstairs, the voices of a hushed argument following her as she went.

In Galloway's garden, Amy walked back along the path, looking at the broken fountain spouts, the cracks in the paving stones where the weeds were pushing through. Perhaps her dad was right, maybe the forgotten things, details like this, could give her a better picture of her captor. Escape wasn't her priority. She knew that already, otherwise she'd have punched in the code at the gates and gone running towards the main road. No, she was still here because she couldn't leave Mia. If knowing your enemy really was the key to escape, then it might also be the key to negotiations. Galloway wanted something from her; that was why she was here. Well that worked both ways.

If Amy May was to get her friend back, then her priority right now was to find out as much as possible about Andy Galloway.

SCARLET'S ROOM
NO. 12

BANG!

The door slammed open. Marge was standing there, her face a picture of war in motion.

'Scarlet. A word.'

The change in Scarlet was as sudden as Marge's appearance. Her eyes narrowed and her tone was spiked with arrogance. 'Go ahead.'

'Outside.'

Scarlet was on her feet, but she stood her ground. 'What for? Are you going to tell me we're suddenly making paedo-flicks? Do you know how old this girl is?'

Marge lurched forward and grabbed Scarlet by the arm. 'Out. Side!'

As Scarlet was dragged out, Mia heard her yell, 'Hey, get your hands off me!'

Marge looked back into the room. 'And you,' she pointed a finger at Mia. 'You stay right where you are.'

Mia heard their footsteps retreated down the corridor, a door open and close.

Prostitutes? Porno Movies? How had she ended up

here? And how was she going to get out of it? Was Scarlet arguing her case, making that old hag see sense?

Mia got up, walked to the door, then back again. She sat down, then got immediately back to her feet.

What if the old woman couldn't be convinced? Why was she even relying on this girl? Why wasn't she taking the chance to run?

She opened the door a crack and peered through. She could hear voices, but they were no longer ranting, and the main voice was Marge. It didn't sound like Scarlet was arguing back at all.

She bit her lip, pulled the door wider and slipped out.

She could still hear voices, but the hall was clear. Mia crept along to the stairs. They were clear too. With a quick look behind, she ran down as quickly and quietly as she could. At the first landing she noticed a woman going into one of the rooms, but her back was to Mia and she didn't give her a second glance.

Mia continued down the next stairway to the ground floor, the hallway and the door she'd came in through. The way out.

Less than halfway, she heard footsteps behind her. She jumped, convinced it was Marge coming to get her. Instead, there was a tall girl, about the same age as Scarlet. She slipped past with a quick, 'Excuse me,' then trotted down the rest of the stairs.

The next thing Mia heard was the same girl saying, 'Can you do the door?'

A male voice. 'You back before midnight?'

The girl laughed. 'What do you think?'

'I don't wanna know.'

Mia crouched down to see a man walk to the door and unlock the catch with a key attached to his belt by an extendable cable. As soon as the girl was out, he closed the door and walked back into the lobby. Mia crept down one more step to see him sit in the chair near the phone.

She should have known! He'd been there earlier, hadn't he? Taking calls. How could she have forgotten? At the time, she thought he was just part of the welcoming party, someone to make sure they got her into the building so the driver and bodyguard could get back in the car. She hadn't realised he was sitting at a permanent post. Unless she was ready to fight her way out, this wasn't really an option.

She climbed back upstairs.

On the first floor landing she looked about. Just like the floor above, there was a long corridor and doors leading off either side. She tried the first handle gently. It was locked, but from inside she heard a woman shout, 'Two minutes.'

Mia quickly turned tail and shot back upstairs, checked the coast was clear, and went back into Scarlet's room.

The place was exactly as she'd left it. Panic growing, she tried to think whether there were any other options. Only one came to mind: the window.

Mia pulled open the curtains and looked out. With the gloom of the hallway, it was a shock to see that it was still daylight outside. The sun was low, and afternoon was fading to evening, but she could clearly see the back yard, a wall, and beyond that, and to either side, rows of ancient terraces with brickwork crumbling, bin bags clogging the back lanes. A culture shock from her own beige-brick three-bedroom detached with gardens and garage, the pond, trampoline and apple tree.

Time was running out. She unlatched the window and yanked it up. The window lifted, but only a few centimetres. In that moment, Mia was hit by the horrible thought that it was somehow fixed, or fitted with child locks, so that it couldn't open any more. In desperation, she slipped her fingers under the window and gripped the frame from below. With two hefty pulls, it gave a scrape and shot up. Her exit was wide open.

Mia didn't hesitate. She bent low, put one leg through the open window, held the sill for support, and squeezed out through the opening.

'I wouldn't do that if I were you.'

The door closed – Mia hadn't even heard it open – and there was Scarlet. She was alone; no sign of Marge.

'Seriously, Mia,' she said. 'I know why you're doing this, but they've already thought of that. If you drop down into the back yard, you'll have about ten seconds to get to the other side and scale a six foot wall topped with broken glass and razor wire. Otherwise, you'll have the dogs on you.' Scarlet slumped back on to her bed and spoke to the ceiling. 'Face it, babe. For now, you're stuck here.'

Mia paused. She looked down into the yard, and she saw that Scarlet was right – the wall surrounding the small, grubby back yard was topped with slapped-on concrete that had been set with jagged broken bottles. Somewhere along the line, someone had decided this was not enough, so just above this, Mia could see the spirals of grey wire, each and every curl loaded with razor-sharp metal teeth.

Everything about this place made Mia feel weak. 'I can't stay here,' she said.

'And you can't escape.' Scarlet paused. 'At least not that way.' With a sigh, she said, 'Why don't you come back in, babe? Maybe we can get you out a different way, but for now, come back inside.'

Mia looked down, judging the distance: the run she'd have, the height of the wall. 'I can make it.'

'One girl tried six months ago. She only slipped once. You wouldn't believe the state of her face. Honestly, Mia. It's not worth the risk. Not when you can walk out of the front door.'

'Walk out?'

'You just have to do what they say.'

Mia took a final look at the yard below. The wall was high, but there was space to run at it, gather speed. In the gym, she could vault higher. But in the gym, there wasn't razor wire and broken glass ready to lacerate her skin.

As she turned back to the room, she asked, 'What do they want me to do?'

Scarlet sighed. 'They want you down the corridor.'

So this is it. Her thoughts flashed back to Dan, the excitement of a first kiss, sneaking moments together, building trust, the butterflies and uncertainty.

But here, there was only fear.

'That's where the studio is,' said Scarlet. She got up from the bed and went to the wardrobe. She fished about and pulled something out. 'I'm sorry to be the one to do this, Mia, but as we're the same size . . .' She held out a red lace bodice. 'They want you to take this in with you.'

Mia felt sick. She came away from the window, weakly taking the bodice, holding it like it was infected. 'I don't think I can. I mean, I can't.' There was a touch of panic in her voice. 'I can't do this.'

Scarlet moved closer, a hand touching Mia's shoulder, her voice little more than a whisper. 'You can, babe. You can, because there's no other choice.'

Mia shook her head and tried to pull away. She looked once more to the window, then the door. There must be another way out of here.

But Scarlet held her firm. 'Listen to me.'

Mia wouldn't meet her eyes. She just looked from the bodice to the floor of a room she should know nothing about. She could feel her own tears, feel herself shaking. 'I can't do this.'

Scarlet continued to hold her firm. 'Shhh. You can, babe. Just go in there, and do what they tell you to. It'll be over before you know it.'

GALLOWAY'S OFFICE
WEST HALL MANOR

Amy stepped into Galloway's office. He was behind the desk, but got straight to his feet to greet her.

'Amy! Good to see you again. Come on in.'

Amy was taking in as much about the office as she could – the shelves, the closed blinds at the window. There was a wooden easel by the side of the desk with a sheet covering the canvas. On the desk itself, over papers and folders, there were several books, all on art history, one of which was lying open.

'You've had something to eat, yes?'

She answered with a simple, 'Yes.'

'Ah, she's a fine chef is our Alice. More than just a cook. She keeps the whole house spick and span.' He indicated one of the seats facing the desk. 'Please, sit down.'

Amy sat.

Galloway seemed in a very jovial mood, clapping his hands together as he returned to his own side of the desk. 'Did Michelle give you the full tour? It's not a bad old place, is it? Costs a bloody fortune to run, but it has a certain wow factor, you know what I mean? A man in my position has to maintain a certain air.'

'The air of an arms dealer.'

'Oh, Amy, Amy. Please. I like to think there's a lot more to me than shipping a few guns about.'

His smile showed a glint of white, capped teeth, and Amy didn't trust its sincerity for a second. 'What do you want?'

Galloway leaned back on his chair, an elbow on the armrest, fingers touching his chin in thought.

'I want you to work for me.'

Amy tried to hold her composure, but she couldn't help her eyebrows arching. 'Are you for real?'

'I'm offering a straight deal, Amy. You work for me, you can reap the rewards. The house, the lifestyle, that's only part of it. You can have money in your pocket, prospects.'

'I don't care about any of that. I'm not interested.'

Galloway seemed to weigh this up.

'Well, I sort of expected that. Very noble. A good moral decision. Tell me, do you think morals are important, Amy?'

Amy chose not to reply. She recalled her father's words: *Experience helps you to fight those knee-jerk moral reactions . . .*

'I'm curious,' said Galloway. 'Do you think it's more important to do what is right, than look after number one?'

'Of course,' she replied, but she thought about why her father had helped train his own captors.

Again, Galloway made a point of weighing things up, then said, 'Do you think it's more important to do what is right, than look after someone else? Someone you care about?'

He had her attention now.

'What's on offer is only part of the deal. Obviously, I'd like you to choose to work for me, but to help your decision, there are also certain . . . consequences, if you don't.' He pulled the laptop closer and tapped a key. From the ceiling, on the far side of the room, a projector screen unrolled. On the screen was a projection of Galloway's laptop. The pointer moved around the screen and opened a folder. There was a single file inside.

'Do you remember when I said things were going to get unpleasant?' He clicked on the file. 'I didn't mean for you.'

The movie player filled the screen.

'It will take a moment to establish the link, but I assure you, what you are about to see, is live.'

The studio was two rooms knocked into one. It was decorated to look half like an apartment, with coffee table, leather sofa and pictures on the wall, and half like a bedroom with a double bed, shelves, bedside cabinets and even reading lamps. In the area between the two halves were tripods, lights and cables. There was a small table with a laptop computer, and next to that, a trolley with gels, bottles and packets of wet wipes.

There were two men in the room. The younger one, overweight with long, greasy hair, was setting up the camera, while the other, bald, muscular and about as old as Marge, locked the door.

'Sit down.' He indicated a chair against the blank wall between the two sets. His voice was tight, like he was talking with a band around his neck – the rough sound of a lifelong smoker.

The chair was simple – wooden backed, wooden seat – but something about it made Mia's heart go in to overdrive.

'Sit in the chair.' It was a command. Pure, simple, without threat or compromise.

Barely able to catch her breath, Mia walked over to the chair and sat. She held the red lace bodice limply on her lap.

The man with the greasy, long hair approached her, put some kind of meter up to her face while the old man adjusted the lights.

Long hair returned to the laptop. 'Good to go.'

And that was when the older man told Mia what he expected her to do.

Mia sat there, trying not to look about the room, trying not to image what went on in here, and listened. She nodded once to indicate she understood. The old man withdrew and the two of them watched the screen of the laptop. They seemed to stand there for an age, until finally, the younger one nodded. 'Streaming.'

The old man stepped aside, his eyes on Mia. He simply pointed a finger to indicate the time was now.

Mia sniffed and looked directly at the camera.

'Hello, Amy.' For a moment, everything went out of her mind, all the things she'd been instructed to say. She glanced at the old man. He was staring at her, his expression stern. She took a breath and pushed on. 'I know you're watching this. I can't tell you where I am, but it's nothing like where you are, that's for sure.' She felt her voice break up, and didn't bother to wipe the tears. 'I can't get out. It's a whole row of houses. Prostitutes in most. But in here, they make films, and they've made it clear what I'll be doing.' She briefly held up the bodice. 'And what I'll be wearing when they film me.'

Her hands were shaking so much that she dropped the bodice. The sudden movement of the old man took her by surprise and she flinched back in the chair. But all he did was snatch the bodice out of shot and pass it back to her.

She took it, then noticed the man with the greasy hair, staring at her image on the laptop's screen, nodding, smiling. He glanced over, held up his hand and whirled his finger in a circle: keep going.

Mia sniffed again. 'I don't know what it is they want you to do, Amy. All I know is they think you're important. Special.' She wiped her nose with the back of her hand. 'But if you don't help them out, then they're going to make me . . . do . . . things.'

She could barely get the rest of her words out, choking on tears, making herself almost incoherent. The old man growled something. Mia just nodded, and managed to regain control to plead to the camera, 'I don't want to stay here, Amy. If you could see what I can see. If I told you what they've got in mind . . . please . . .'

GALLOWAY'S OFFICE
WEST HALL MANOR

Galloway cut the video short and closed the window. He sat back, his eyes watching Amy.

Seconds passed. Galloway said nothing. Amy said nothing.

She wanted to think it was a trick, that maybe Mia was here, in the house somewhere, that she was fine and this was just a test or some kind of joke . . .

But the bodies of the people who had kidnapped them that morning were no joke, nor were the bullets that killed them.

So no, there was no doubt. No doubt at all. Wherever Mia was, she believed they meant what they said – and so did Amy.

Seconds turned to minutes. Still Amy couldn't talk.

Galloway's voice broke the silence. 'I don't think we need to see any more, do you?'

Amy wanted to speak, but all she could manage was a shake of her head.

Galloway remained still. 'I give you my word, Amy. If you work for me, Mia will not be harmed. She won't be touched, filmed, or made to feel uncomfortable in any way.'

'Your word?' Amy felt weak. 'That's supposed to mean something, is it?'

Galloway's eyes were firm. 'In my line of work, young lady, my word means everything. When I give my word, I keep to it.'

'You send her to a place like that. Tie her to a chair . . .'

'I didn't see any ropes.'

'She's sitting there, scared witless, talking about porn movies. *You* put her there, and you expect me to trust you? So what's she doing now, just waiting to hear from you?'

'Pretty much. She's safe. She's clean, and she's not working. She'll stay in her room until I call back. You may not like how I operate, Amy, but I'll make things crystal clear. This is a straightforward business proposition. You agree to work for me and Mia leaves that place. I have another house in a better part of town. A place I use when I don't want to travel all the way out here. It has all mod cons. She can stay in comfort, where she'll be safe.'

'You mean locked up?'

'Well she won't be able to walk out the door, not at this stage, but she'll not be where she is right now. Isn't that the main thing?'

'Or you could let her go. I'll do what you want if you let her go.' Because she would. She knew it now. She couldn't allow anything to happen to her friend.

Galloway shook his head. 'Can't do that. At least not yet, but it's certainly something we can build towards. You work for me, and you'll have taken the first step towards that goal.' He tipped his head a touch. 'It's a way out of this, Amy. It's certainly a better deal than your kidnappers got.'

'You mean better than a bullet.'

Galloway didn't falter. He gave a nod and a straight, 'Yes.'

Amy was suddenly aware that she was twisting her hands together, rubbing her fingers, squeezing the knuckles. She managed to control it, hold the sides of the chair, but only for a moment.

Finally, she looked up. 'So what do you want me to do?'

Mia stepped back into her room to find Scarlet sitting on the bed.

'How did it go?'

'Well I didn't have to . . . I just had to talk to the camera, say what was going to happen, show this . . . thing.'

Scarlet got up and hugged her, kissing the side of her head. 'You see, babe. Didn't I tell you it was going to be okay?' She took back the bodice and cast it on the bed. 'And this "thing", as you call it, cost nearly forty quid.' She actually smiled. 'It works for me – goes with the hair.'

But Mia had other concerns. 'Did you know that's what they had in mind?'

'Marge said you wouldn't be hurt . . . she didn't give any details, didn't say *why* they wanted to film you.'

Mia heard the question in Scarlet's voice, but she couldn't answer. She didn't want to break down, but she couldn't help herself. And as she did, Scarlet held her close, whispering gentle words that everything was going to be all right.

Slowly, Mia calmed. She pulled away. 'It's to do with my friend Amy. They want to show her what would happen if she doesn't do what they want.'

'So long as your show reel works, you'll be fine.' Scarlet smiled brightly, but Mia wasn't convinced.

'What if it doesn't? Are they planning another one? Something a little stronger?'

Scarlet didn't reply. She didn't need to; it was written right across her face.

A surge of sick panic filled Mia. She looked again to the window. 'I've got to get out of here.' She was talking to herself more than Scarlet. 'This isn't going to work.'

'Give it a chance.'

Mia shook her head. 'You don't know Amy. She won't be blackmailed.'

'She won't protect a friend?'

'She won't be forced into doing something she doesn't want to do.'

She wouldn't have sat in front of a camera either. Mia knew that. Amy wouldn't fall to pieces, saying things she'd been ordered to, just to put pressure on a friend.

Mia became so focussed on what Amy would and wouldn't do, she barely heard Scarlet's tone of disgust. 'So she'll just expect you to stop here and get on with it, eh? Some friend.'

But Mia knew exactly what Amy would expect, and Scarlet's tone of disgust was nothing compared to what Amy would say right now. She'd be yelling at her to take a stand. Amy would expect her to fight.

Keeping these thoughts to herself, Mia stepped towards the window and looked out.

'Don't even think about it,' said Scarlet. 'Honestly. The dogs down there are mastiffs. Canary mastiffs, if that means anything to you. If they catch you, they'll rip you to shreds.'

The late summer evening was finally at an end. Dusk was cutting in, and despite what Scarlet was saying, there wasn't any sign of dogs down in the back yard. Maybe they were somewhere else. Maybe they were asleep. Maybe . . .

Mia looked back into the room, at Scarlet.

. . . Maybe she was lying. After all, she worked here, coming and going as she pleased . . .

'Don't do it, babe.' Scarlet approached, her hand held out.

Why should she trust this girl? Because she called her babe? Because she tried to comfort her before she went into the studio? It hadn't made any difference though, had it? She still had to go through it, to sit there and do what she was told. And who gave her that thing to wear? Who was trying to convince her to stay here, talking about Marge and dogs and no way out? What was this? Good cop, bad cop?

Everything about Scarlet was fake, from her hair to the points on her nails, so why trust her sincerity? Why believe a word she said.

And yeah, Amy would *fight*.

Scarlet took another step forward, her smile kind, trustworthy, but Mia saw through it. She saw control, intent, and in that single moment her anger flashed to boiling point. She turned side on and threw out her right foot in a powerful standing-roundhouse – right to the side of Scarlet's head.

It might not have been as good as Amy taught her, but it did the trick. Scarlet was taken by surprise and knocked clean off her feet. As soon she hit the floor, her expression changed. Was it shock? Something more? Anger? Fury? Aggression? Mia saw all three and prepared for retaliation.

Scarlet jumped back up and came at her with bared teeth and an open hand aimed right at Mia's face. Mia blocked the slap, knocked it aside, and struck under her chin with a fist. She followed up immediately, elbowing Scarlet in the chest, just enough to knock her back to give her the room to step forward, spin and strike with the back of a fist.

Scarlet didn't have time to scream; she simply fell against the door and crumpled to the floor. But the noise would have someone coming. Mia had to act quickly. She heaved the window open and put one foot onto the sill.

A hand grabbed her ankle. Scarlet was there, face red with blood, eyes wild. 'Don't do it, Mia.'

'Get your hand off me, or I swear I'll . . .'

Below, the sounds of dogs barking. Mia took a glance, in time to see the most monstrous, snarling black hulk of a dog. A bulk of muscle with a wrinkled snout and short, stubby ears. It caught sight of her and jumped up, clearing the ground by several feet.

A second later, she was on the floor of the room, Scarlet having yanked her back inside.

Mia couldn't believe what she'd just seen. 'Jesus. What are they?'

Scarlet, face still bleeding, shut the window and pulled the curtains.

'I told you. Canary mastiffs – *Presa Canario*. Ever heard of them? Aggressive, powerful. You wouldn't stand a chance.' Scarlet checked her nose with her hand. 'Oh, nice one, babe.'

'Don't call me that!' Mia was still raging, but suddenly she saw just how shaken Scarlet was. She actually looked terrified, and not because of Mia.

'You were telling the truth,' said Mia, doubt fading from her voice. 'About the dogs – you were telling the truth.'

'Oh, so now you believe me, eh?' said Scarlet, checking her nose again. 'And even for mastiffs, they're big. The dogs are injected with steroids, like the meathead who owns them. Just because I work here, Mia, doesn't mean I go along with every part of the business. I do my bit, I get my pay, and I put most of it in the bank, because believe it or not, little girl, I don't want to be here until I'm old and grey. And the last thing I want to leave here with is the memory of a fifteen-year-old girl torn to bits by dogs.'

Mia was breathing hard. 'I still think I could have made it.'

'Yeah? And what if you had? What do you think they're going to do to your friend if you get away?'

'So what should I do?'

Scarlet turned to the mirror, cleaning up her nose with a tissue. 'My advice is that you sit it out, give it time, and wait to hear what they come back with. If she's any kind of friend she'll do whatever they ask to keep you out of that studio.'

The dog was still barking down below, and by the sounds of it, it had been joined by another. There was a crash of a bin lid and a deep male voice yelling at them to, 'Shut yer noise!'

Mia got up and sat on the edge of the bed near Scarlet. 'Are you okay?'

'It's only a slight bleed. I'm just glad it's not broken.' She dabbed at it some more. 'Where did you learn that stuff? You do karate or something?'

Mia looked down. 'Amy taught me.'

Galloway tapped the table, his tone a touch lighter – there was even a hint of a smile.

'When you snatched that gun from my hand, Amy, I knew you were something special. You made a decision in a microsecond and took a huge risk. You might not have the killer instinct to pull the trigger, but you do have a very strong desire to survive, to escape.' He smiled. 'Hopefully not from here.'

'What do you want?'

'Let me ask you something. You do all this gymnastic stuff, competitions and the like: you like winning, don't you?'

'Of course.'

'But does it bring in the money? Oh, I'm sure it does if you're that one in the million, bring back a gold medal, get the sponsorship deals. But let's face facts, Amy, at fifteen, you've missed out on these Olympics by what – a matter of months? When the next Games come around, you'll be nineteen. Is that too old?' He steepled his fingers, resting them on his chin. 'You tell me.'

Amy's face was tight as she tried to contain her anger.

She refused to bite, and repeated her question, 'What do you *want*?'

Galloway paused. He opened his hands and spread them face down on the desk. 'I need a thief, Amy.'

'A what?'

'Let me rephrase that: I need an *exceptional* thief – someone with skills to get places that other thieves can't. I need someone at the peak of their ability. In short, Amy, I need you.'

'For what? Stealing guns and ammo?'

'Oh, I think you're much too special for that.' Galloway considered for a moment. 'I deal in a lot of things, Amy. Stocks, shares, medical equipment, medicines, even foreign aid. But I also deal in fine art. Do you like art?'

Amy tried to keep her expression firm, giving nothing away. But she could feel curiosity pushing its way in. 'I can't say I've really thought about it.'

'Do you know the difference between art and arms, Amy?'

'Paintings don't kill people.'

Galloway smiled. 'Very droll. No. I'm a businessman, my dear. And I'm far too long in the tooth to lose any sleep over a bunch of backstreet morons playing cowboys and Indians like children. No, the problem with guns and ammo is there are only so many routes to the consumer – the *buyer*. But with artwork, thanks to the internet, I've got the whole world. If I dealt only in arms, I could get by, live fairly comfortably. But if

I sell the right painting, I can be *very* comfortable for several years. And to allay those morals of yours, most of the paintings I deal with are already stolen – hence the very tasty market value.'

Amy couldn't help herself. 'I don't get you.'

Galloway picked up the phone, hitting a single key. After a moment, he said, 'Richard, could you bring some drinks through to my office . . . No, just soft drinks. Yes, lemonade's fine. Plenty of ice.'

He put the phone down and stood up. 'Let me put this in simple terms.' He removed the sheet from the easel. The small canvas was covered in bold brushstrokes: a prairie with pendulous clouds looming overhead. 'This is a painting by Turner. If you know your art history, you might appreciate why this has a certain value. The fact that it is said to be a perfect example of his use of transparent colours to capture light adds more, but here's the real value – this painting was stolen from a private collection a short time ago.'

The live video of Mia was still fresh in Amy's mind, making it difficult to focus. 'Why does that make a difference?'

'Well, imagine this particular painting was hanging in the Tate in London, or in the Louvre in Paris. It would still be a valuable painting, no doubt about that, but it would have a very *low* black-market price tag. That's because the chances of stealing it are so unlikely. It's too well protected. It's not that collectors don't want it, it's more that it isn't really on offer. As far as the black-market goes, collectors are opportunists – they don't waste time on what they can't have. Instead, they go for what *is* available. So once a painting has been stolen, its underworld value soars. Collectors who want it will let the word out they are interested, and the wheels of the black-market begin to turn. Only sometimes, the new owner isn't so keen on selling. They see it as an investment, see? And the longer they have the painting in their possession, the black-market value begins to grow.'

Galloway hit a key on the laptop and the screen behind him changed from the desktop to a painting – at first, it appeared as nothing more than blue and white smears on a black background.

'This painting was stolen about fifteen years ago from a private collection in Northern Spain. It has always been believed to be by an artist called Braque, which alone makes it very valuable. Have you ever heard the name?'

Amy looked at the picture. It still looked like a total mess. 'No.'

'Oh, he's a big name. At least in the art world. I could bore you with words like expressionism and cubism, but let's just get straight to the point. Perhaps you have heard of his partner, a man called Pablo Picasso.'

Amy sat up. 'Yes. At least, I've heard the name.'

'And yet you know nothing of art,' said Galloway. He leaned forward. 'That's the difference! In art circles, Braque and Picasso go hand in hand, but when you talk to the layman, only one name stands out. Guess whose paintings sell for most?'

The question was rhetorical, so Amy said nothing.

Galloway just nodded. 'Exactly. The problem with these two is that they worked very closely together. They began to experiment with movement and the viewing angles of the artist to a degree that it's almost impossible to tell what it was they were supposed to be painting. But more importantly, they worked so closely together that until recently, many paintings have been the cause of argument among experts who cannot decide who painted what.'

The door opened. Richard, the barman, walked in carrying a tray. Without a word, he put it down and poured two glasses of lemonade.

Galloway continued. 'So here's this painting, not in a gallery with a hundred thousand pounds worth of security keeping it safe, but sold on the black-market and re-housed in another private collection, specifically the penthouse of a building in North London. Imagine the owner's surprise when it is announced that experts have uncovered some letters, correspondence between the two artists, where this particular painting is mentioned by name, leaving no doubt that it was not painted by Braque at all. It is, in fact . . .'

He trailed off, leaving Amy to say, 'It's by Picasso.'

Galloway took a sip of lemonade. 'You can probably guess what this does to the value.'

'I'd guess it goes up.'

'It *rockets* up, Amy. What's more, people know it's out there. Even the original owner, the person it was stolen *from*, has offered money to get it back. But the current owner isn't going to release it until he gets an offer he considers worthy of a lost Picasso, which is a big risk considering he's sitting on a stolen painting that so many people are suddenly interested in. As buyers increase their offers, word spreads, which can attract the attention of bounty hunters: people working for insurance companies, who make it their business to track down these paintings and retrieve them. And that makes potential buyers nervous, so they continue raising their offers in the hope that the owner will cave in. Well, I happen to know one such buyer who isn't prepared to wait. He's got the money – lots of money – and he *really* wants this painting. And that, my dear, is where you come in.'

'Me?'

'You're going to steal it.'

The door gently clicked shut as the barman left.

Galloway smiled at Amy's silence. 'Oh, don't worry. You'll have plenty of training. If you're not one hundred per cent capable of getting it, you won't go.'

'Why me? If you've already managed to get that one,' she motioned to the Turner.

'Actually, that is painting number two. The first theft was flawless. The second had a few problems. To cut a long story short, it appears I've got some competition. And I don't like second place, Amy. I don't like losing. Ever. That's how I've managed to build up a lifestyle like this, and I'm not going to have it taken from me. I need someone who has that same work ethic, but also has the skills to succeed. In short: you. You certainly have the talent and you have a natural motivation to win, to beat your rivals. But, now you have a little more to drive you. If you complete the job . . .' he held his palms up. 'Mia will be safe, and we can negotiate further.'

'And if I don't?'

'Let's not go there, eh? Let's agree it's not an option.'

Amy's instinct was to tell him to shove it, but she held back. She turned her attention back to the painting. It was nothing more than streaks of meaningless colour.

'How can such a mess be so valuable?'

'Where you see mess, others see perfection. Oddly enough, the subject of the painting itself.' Galloway rose to his feet and approached the painting. He looked closely. 'Picasso was a master of his craft. Be assured, there isn't a single random mark on that canvas.'

'Yes, but what is it supposed to be?'

'She's a ballet dancer. See, here, the vertical marks indicating the leg, and here, the curve of her other leg outstretched behind her, the arched back and neck curving up.'

Amy's intake of breath caused Galloway to pat the table and say, 'Ah, you see it now, do you? You recognise the pose? I believe it has the same name in your area of expertise.'

'Arabesque,' said Amy.

'Correct. Otherwise known as the perfect form, or the perfection of balance and muscular tone, painted by a master who achieved perfection in his own craft. And also the title of the piece: *Arabesque*. Quite like you, in a way.'

'What?'

'An Olympic-standard gymnast, a cool head in a situation where others would panic or fall apart. Balance and power. That's you, Amy May. A living, breathing, arabesque. And that's why I want you. You could be the perfect thief, Amy. You could be the *best*.'

The artist sat on a stool, working. He was nineteen years old and painfully thin. Every now and then he'd brush his long dark hair back over his ears as he worked. His glasses didn't fit quite right, slipping down to the end of his nose, and his goatee was so sparse it looked a waste of time ever growing one.

The studio was bright with natural light coming through three large, north-facing windows. The walls were covered in posters, photographs and finished artwork. There was a double-sink area with a kettle nearby, several dirty mugs and a drying rack to the right. Every other available space was crammed with books, paints and boxes of other equipment.

The young man didn't use an easel, instead he was seated at a tilted draftsman's desk. The horizontal straight-edge had been removed, leaving a massive working area. Blocks were fixed to the surface, holding the stretched canvas firmly in place. Surrounding the canvas were photographs, all of the same painting. Some were close-up detail, others showed the piece as a whole and some from a distance. The painting that appeared in each and every photograph was currently being replicated on the canvas. It was the same piece that Amy May had seen just a few hours before.

In the background, music played. Not gentle, classical tones often associated with artists; this was grinding, dark metal – turned down low, making it sound all the more malevolent and distorted.

There were footsteps outside and three short knocks on the door, a pause, then a fourth. The artist called out, 'Just a minute,' and continued to work. He moved his eyes repeatedly from the photographs to the fine line of white paint he was applying, slowly, accurately following a line that was probably knocked out in a second by the original artist.

Finally, he sat up and placed the brush down. He stared at the painting, then the photographs, back and forth.

Satisfied, he got up and unlocked the door.

The man who stepped into the room and locked the door behind him, was of a similar age. He was lean, toned with muscle. A single stud earring in his left ear and light stubble on his chin. But there was something else. His eyes. They were unusually wide; enough to make his pale grey irises float on their whites as he stared, unflinching, at the artist.

'Alex,' said the artist. He nodded a greeting.

'How's it going, Kyle?'

Kyle returned to his desk. 'The first part is nearly complete. I've made good time on this one, considering the size. Picasso often worked small, but not in this case.'

Alex walked into the room, to the benches. He passed the books and the boxes and stopped at a large glass vivarium and tapped it with his finger. Inside, several Black Emperor scorpions ignored him.

'So when will it be ready?' he asked.

'Should be done by the end of the week.'

'I thought you said these acrylic paints dry fast.'

'It's a bit more complicated than the others. Acrylic paints do dry faster than oils, but the finish I need to put on it to make it *look* like oils takes four to five hours to dry. After that, I need to bake the canvas for the same length of time and then unpin it from the frame.'

Alex turned. 'Unpin it? Why?'

'Because unlike the others, this painting is going to get removed from its frame when it's stolen. The tacks will be taken out, leaving tiny holes in the canvas. If Galloway knows anything about old paintings, he'll realise the canvas isn't nearly as old as it should be.'

Alex approached the desk. 'How come?'

'Because the holes will be clean. Baking the canvas cracks the glaze, but it doesn't solve the problem of the holes made by the tacks.' He pointed to one of the photographs on the edge of the desk. 'Look here. See that?'

Alex looked. 'I just see a hole in some old canvas.'

'Yeah, well I see a lot more. I see the way the fibres are punched down and discoloured at their edges. I can see that the pins have oxidised over time, staining those fibres, leaving their mark. So once I've applied the glaze, then baked it, I'm going to unpin it and airbrush the fibres around those holes, making it look like time has taken its toll and the tacks have been in there for years.'

'How on earth do you come up with stuff like that?'

Kyle looked closely at the line he'd just completed. 'Because I'm obsessive about detail. And if I don't get it right, we don't get paid.'

Amy had been up since the early hours. The sky was grey outside and the landscape alien, brushed with wisps of mists like the remnants of a fallen cloud. The sun would soon burn through, but the miles of farmland turned Amy cold: a reminder of how far she was from home.

Her door was unlocked and the house was quiet as she made her way downstairs to the main room, where she sat for too long, watching herself and Mia on the news. There was no need to record or rewind: news channels were running the story every twenty minutes, relishing the drama of the burnt-out house and the three bodies found within, discussing that if the bodies did not belong to the missing girls, then who were they?

There were questions about the woman who had been renting the house from her own parents and speculation about the man said to be her boyfriend. Amy felt a chill cut right up her spine when photographs of Carla and Micky were shown. The third body had yet to be identified.

But the photographs that dogged each and every

report were of Amy and Mia. Amy recognised the school portrait of Mia; it was the one framed in her mum's front room. But there were several photographs of Amy. There was a similar portrait, but as well as this, one station showed a shot of her balanced on the beam, taken from the opening to a performance. Another showed her holding a trophy. And the reports kept bringing the story back to her potential career, her promise as a gymnast, barely giving Mia a mention. Mia, who was just as much of a victim in all of this – *more*, in fact. She wouldn't have been taken at all if it wasn't for Amy, and now, out of the two of them, she was the one in the darkest place.

As the news reports blended into each other, Amy wondered what Mia's mum would be making of it all, seeing her daughter being portrayed as only second best in the kidnap stakes, being made to feel that her daughter didn't quite have the edge needed to make great morning television.

And what would she be thinking about her daughter's whereabouts? That her daughter was locked up somewhere in a cellar with tape across her mouth, or tied to a bed in some run-down house with bare floorboards and torn-off wallpaper.

One day, it would come out. One day, she'd find out exactly where Mia had been taken. And depending on whether Amy measured up to Galloway's expectations, she would either discover what her daughter had been saved from, or find out what she'd been forced to do.

Which brought Amy right back to the decision in

hand. But was there really a decision to be made? Did she have a choice?

She tried to keep her mind fixed on the idea that she didn't, that the decision was forced upon her, and she simply had to get Mia out of there. But her thoughts strayed. They strayed towards excitement, and a secret buzz that Galloway had seen something in her, that he was convinced she could do the job. That she really could be the best.

And the more she tried to shut those thoughts away, the more they played and mocked in her mind until eventually, she got up, switched off the television and left the room.

That was when she passed the library and noticed the computer.

She paused. The door was half open, and the computer's screensaver was bouncing something around the black background.

She should go in.

To do what? Contact the police? How? Drop them an email? Send them a tweet? Change her Facebook status?

Amy May is locked up in some house in the country. LOL.

But she wasn't locked up, was she? She'd already been told about the code, that she could walk out at any time.

She could tell them about Mia, but what did she actually know? She could say that they were both alive, but safe and well didn't really cover it. So what else? Should she put what lay in the balance for Mia? Would that kick people into gear, or make things worse? What would happen if Galloway found out?

Amy just stood there, pausing, wasting time. Why? Was it that deep down, she actually liked Galloway's offer more than she wanted to admit?

The computer sat there, screensaver continuing its endless bounce around the screen. And back home, so many people worrying about her, about Mia.

Maybe if she put something ambiguous – something subtle, like a smiley or a wink – just something to hint that she was here, that she wasn't lying back and taking it, that she was prepared to do something.

Because in a way, she was.

Wasn't she?

With a quick look over her shoulder, Amy slipped into the room.

She approached the computer, moved the chair to one side and moved the mouse to cancel the screensaver.

The bouncing ball was replaced with a simple box window: LOG ON.

There was nothing else. No user list, no icons, no space to type.

She moved the mouse again, clicked about.

Nothing. No pointer. Nothing to click.

She tapped the keyboard. Nothing. She even pressed CTRL, ALT and DELETE, but the screen didn't change.

A voice from behind her said, 'You need to scan your thumb to log in.'

Amy jumped. Michelle was standing there. 'You didn't really think you could just walk in here and send an email, did you? The phones are protected too. Fancy some breakfast?'

Salinger arrived at the house a short time later. He parked the car and, as he got out, he noticed Michelle standing at the door with a polite smile on her face.

'Looks like it's going to be the perfect morning for it,' she said.

Salinger took a brief look at the cloudless sky. The morning was cool with a slight breeze, but it was going to be a scorcher of a day. He grabbed a large holdall from the boot and walked towards Michelle.

Ignoring her question, he grunted, 'Is she up?'

Michelle's smile faded. 'She is. She's in the garden.'

'And Galloway?'

'Mr Galloway is away on business. I've no idea if he'll be back today.'

Jake didn't care one way or the other; it was really just something to say. 'No matter. I don't need to see him again until I know whether or not this girl is capable of doing the job.'

He pushed past Michelle and made his way straight through the house.

Michelle followed him to the conservatory. Her voice was light, almost chatty. 'So you know the final painting now?'

Salinger didn't even break his stride as he lied, 'No. Not this time. Not until the last minute. Why, do you?'

Michelle shook her head. 'I'll be the last to know.'

At the doors to the garden, Salinger paused. He could see the figure sitting on the bench about thirty yards away. His initial reaction was surprise at just how young she looked.

'That's her, is it?'

'Yes.'

He huffed disapproval. 'When Galloway said she was a girl, I didn't think he really meant she's just a kid.'

'Fifteen. I've spoken to her a few times,' said Michelle. 'Don't underestimate her. There's something about that girl. Her name is –'

'Amy May. Yeah, I know. She's a gymnast. Big deal. She's also all over the news. What the hell is Galloway thinking?'

Michelle pursed her lips, then in a calm voice she said, '*Mr* Galloway seems to think that she's the best bet to get the painting. Considering what happened with the last one, I'd say he's well within his rights, wouldn't you?'

Salinger didn't even glance her way as he replied, 'Don't even think of questioning my ability, love. Galloway can pick and choose who he likes, but at the end of the day, I'm running the job. If she's not up to it, she doesn't go. I'm not doing time in prison because

Galloway wants to employ little girls who can do a cartwheel.'

'He seems to think she can do more than just gymnastics.'

'Yeah? Like what?'

'Self defence. She has fast, instinctive reactions. He didn't give me the full story, but he reckons she's got training far beyond your average schoolgirl.'

Salinger opened the holdall and pulled out a baseball bat. He turned, his cold, steely eyes fixing on Michelle. 'Well let's see.'

Baseball bat in hand, he strode purposefully towards Amy May.

GARDEN
WEST HALL MANOR

Amy heard footsteps but didn't turn. If it was Michelle wanting to cheer her up, she'd fail. If it was the person who was supposed to work with her, then she'd go through the motions, but she was in no mood for conversation.

A deep, commanding tone from behind said, 'Get up.'

Amy twisted just in time to see a strong, stocky man with short hair and a face packed full of hate. He had a baseball bat in one hand, and without any further warning, he lifted it up, gripping it tight with both fists. There was no doubt what was coming next: creased brow, glaring eyes, the way he held that bat, his shoulder muscles bunched – it all screamed out the simple, irrefutable fact that the man was about to swing that thing, and Amy was the target.

In a heartbeat, she threw herself backwards, out of range of the bat, twisting at the same time to fling herself around and on to her feet.

By which time, the man had indeed taken a swing, a swing that would have taken Amy's head off. He didn't waste any time, just stepped forward and prepared for a second attack.

'What are you . . . ?' Amy didn't get any further.

With no more words, the man took a second swing. Amy jumped back, only just avoiding a blow that had been aimed for her left arm.

'What are you doing?' she screamed.

'You run,' growled her attacker, 'and I'll shoot you. You stand still, I'll break your arms, and then your legs.' He took another step towards her.

Amy's mind was racing. He was heavy and strong, but he was short too, so his centre of gravity was low. The only option was to get that thing off him, because even if he was lying about shooting her, and she took the chance to turn and run, he could throw the bat after her.

To buy a moment of time, Amy feigned shock, doing her best to look terrified. She even lifted up her hands and called out, 'Please, no! I don't know what you want.'

Her attacker grinned, gripped the bat, and prepared to take another swing.

But Amy was ready, and instead of retreating, she shot forward just as the attack came. Her arms hooked over his shoulder and around his neck, her right knee pulled up, as she twisted her body to the left, that same leg wrapping around the man's right thigh and pulling with all her weight, yanking with her arms. She was inside the swing of the bat, and with her own body acting as a human lever, she used her attacker's momentum against him, taking the power from the swing, knocking him off balance, and to the ground.

But she didn't end there. As they fell, she released her right arm, hooked the end of the bat inside her elbow and twisted. The result was a crack of the bat against the ground as it came free, and as she and the man hit the floor, her face was right up to his.

With everything she had, she screamed as close as possible to his ear, felt him flinch, and took the chance to twist away from him, snap up the bat, and get to her feet.

He looked dazed for a moment, but he wasn't injured, and he recovered fast. In the time it took for Amy to grab the bat, he was up and at her. He lurched forward, grabbing her free hand by the wrist, pulled her close and started to twist. If he completed this move, locked her arm behind her back, she knew he'd win.

She also knew a counter measure.

Amy went with the twist, leaping up into a back flip, right over the man's shoulder, changing the pressure from her arm to his.

Again, he was forced to release, and turned ready to come at her again. So Amy adjusted her stance, kept a firm grip on the bat with both hands, ready to take her own swing.

The man crouched, eyes narrow, teeth gritted. 'Come on then!'

Amy swung the bat, but as soon as she moved, she realised he was one step ahead. He came into the swing, just like she had done, deflected the blow with his forearm, grabbed the bat at its hilt and with a firm tug, he whipped it from her hands. His other hand shot out and grabbed the hair at the back of her head.

Amy screeched. Anger – *fury* – at being caught out. Her blood was up, her system was flooded with adrenalin and she was prepared to use every trick at her disposal. Her fingers locked in the shape of a claw, first and middle finger hooked like dragon heads, other fingers curled in tight as her hand shot out. The base of her palm slammed into Salinger's nose, the clawed dragon heads went for his eyes.

The man's hand shot up in defence, but too late. Amy snatched her hand back and followed through with a knee to the groin, an uppercut to his chin and right elbow straight to the throat.

Salinger staggered back, bat held firm. He squinted, then checked his nose, smearing the blood onto the back of his free hand. He was breathing hard, his face was grim, then he held up a hand. 'Okay. Calm down. Jesus!'

He snorted, then spat blood onto the ground. Then he threw the baseball bat aside. 'You pass the test, okay?' He spat again and wiped his mouth, blood sticking to teeth in his grin. 'Galloway said you were something special. I guess maybe he was right, eh?'

Amy just stared, fighting to get her breath back, holding back her energy in case this was some trick, that he was getting ready for another attack.

The man stepped forward, his right arm outstretched, hand open.

'Jake Salinger,' he said. 'Looks like you've earned the right to be my apprentice.'

SCARLET'S ROOM NO. 12

Mia had suffered a night of bad dreams, waking to panic, then fear and worry. Somewhere in the house, someone was arguing, but Mia was too scared to get out of bed. All she could do was lie there, going over and over yesterday's events. Sheer exhaustion pulled her back to sleep, and the next thing she knew, someone was standing over her.

'It's past ten o'clock, babe.' Scarlet had a hand on her shoulder. 'You looked like you could have slept all day.'

Mia blinked and was surprised to see bright daylight streaming in through the gap in the curtains. She looked about the room. It wasn't nearly as squalid as it had been in her dreams, but it was no palace either. Slowly, she pushed her feet to the side of the bed and sat up.

'I don't have any clothes. Just what I'm wearing.'

'Don't worry,' said Scarlet. 'I've got a few things you can borrow until you're sorted out.' She laughed at Mia's face. 'No, it's not *all* red lace and lycra! I'll nip out later on and get you some fresh underwear if you like. Not much else to do.'

'No?' Mia couldn't mask her contempt. 'You're not in the studio?'

Scarlet didn't answer at first. She sat there and watched Mia, then she said, 'I'm not going to give you my life story, Mia, or how I came to be here, but right now, for me, it's keeping my head above water. I do a day in the studio maybe once a week. It's by no means an ideal job, but it pays well, and I get to rent a room in a secure house, at a cheap rate. But today I'm not doing much of anything, so if you want me to, I'll go out and get you a few things. Is that what you'd like?'

Mia nodded. 'I'm sorry I snapped like that. It's just . . .'

'Hey, I know. Life can deal you a rotten hand. Believe me, I know. There was a time when I'd have given anything to have a room like this, so while it might look pretty rough to you, like you've come down a peg or two. To me? I'm on my way up.'

She turned and clicked on a small portable TV in the corner of the room. 'Here you go. You might want to avoid the news channels, though. You and your friend are all over them.'

'So you know all about me, do you?'

'I know enough to keep quiet. So don't ask – it's not worth my life. And I know that until your friend agrees to whatever it is they want from her, we're going to remain room-mates.' She pulled open the top drawer of her dresser. 'There are a few DVDs in here if you want.' Before Mia could comment, she quickly added, 'Not the kind filmed here. Just movies. It might make a long day a bit more bearable. I'll bring you back something to eat, eh?'

Mia had to control a wave of anger, panic and worry. If she was going to get out of here, she'd need to keep wits and strength in top condition. So she feigned a weak smile, nodded and said, 'Thanks. I'd appreciate that.'

As Michelle watched Amy and Salinger her mobile rang.

'Mr Galloway?'

'How's it going? Has Jake taken to our girl yet?'

'Oh, I'd say so. He gave her a quick test in self defence.' Michelle couldn't resist a satisfied smile. 'She nearly wiped the floor with him.'

Galloway's voice shot up an octave. 'Seriously?'

'I saw it with my own eyes.'

His laughter crackled down the phone. 'Like I told you, there's more to that wee girl than meets the eye. What are they doing now?'

'Standing by the East Wing, pulling ropes out of a bag.'

'So they've started the training? Excellent. I've got a few things to take care of, Michelle. Be a doll and keep a close eye on them. Inform me of any problems.'

'And what if she asks about the other girl?'

'I told Marge to hang fire, and that's all I'm going to tell her. It sounds like Mia has settled in, so why spoil a good thing? As far as Amy is concerned, we've upheld our side of the bargain. Tell her we've moved Mia out of there, that she's happy, comfortable and safe. Actually, hold back with "happy" – just tell her she's comfortable. We don't want her to think we're telling porkies, do we?'

Michelle raised an eyebrow. 'No?' She closed the phone. 'She might as well get used to them.'

'We've got a job to do,' said Salinger. He went back to collect his holdall, then pointed forwards and led Amy around the side of the house. As they walked, he asked, 'How much has Galloway told you?'

'Not very much. He showed me the painting.'

Jake raised an eyebrow. 'He did? Did he tell you much about it?'

'He mentioned Picasso, told me why it's worth so much.'

'Have you talked to anyone about it?'

Amy looked about. 'Who's there to talk to?'

Salinger glanced back at the gardens they had left behind. Amy followed his gaze to see Michelle examining one of the bushes.

'Has she asked about it?'

'No.'

'Well she tried questioning me, and she did her best to make it sound like she didn't care one way or the other. So first rule, don't let anyone coerce you into chat about the job.'

'Don't you trust her?'

Salinger started walking again. 'I don't trust anyone. Galloway is convinced there's a leak. He's paranoid at the best of times, but in this case, I think he could be right.'

'Do you think someone else is going for the painting?'

'No. I think someone else is trying to make Galloway look like a fool. They are either trying to humiliate him or break the deal after it's been made. That could be very damaging for someone like Galloway. When you build an empire based on a reputation that your word is your bond, it doesn't bode well to cancel an agreement.'

'I still don't get why he wants me to steal it.'

'Because you might be able to do what other burglars can't. A tall building is a perfect trap for a thief – unless you have a thief who can fly.'

'What?'

'That comes later.' Jake dropped the holdall on the floor, opened it and pulled out two large, coiled climbing ropes, several carabiners and a harness. 'First things first. How are you with climbing?'

Amy stood against the wall, looking directly up at the side of the house. It was only three stories, and to most people her age, it probably looked impossible to scale.

From up on top, Salinger called, 'Below!'

Amy kept still, face down while the ends of two ropes fell, uncoiling and thumping onto the ground by her feet.

'Okay,' he called. 'It's down to you. Tie the ropes like I showed you.'

Amy nodded – not that she needed any instruction from Salinger. Tying a rope to a harness was not something new, but doing it here brought back bitter-sweet memories of camping with her dad. Not only because of the precious times spent with him, but because often Mia had been there too.

As she clipped the rope through a carabiner, she recalled the first time Mia had joined them for a trip out.

Amy had given her a list of clothes she would need. They had even gone together to buy her suitable walking shoes, so with those, plus a padded jacket and combat trousers, she looked every inch the experienced hillwalker as she walked up their driveway – apart from the huge suitcase she was pulling behind her. Amy's dad nearly bust a gut laughing at the size of it.

'Morning,' called Mia. 'Hi, Amy. Jesus, am I glad to set this thing down.' Then she caught on to the stifled giggles. 'What's the matter? What's so funny?'

Amy pulled herself together and gave her dad a dig with her elbow. 'We're camping in the Lake District, Mia. We're not going to a hotel. What have you got in there?'

'Just stuff.'

'It looks like a lot of stuff.'

Reluctantly, Mia opened her case, and neither Amy, nor her dad could contain a second bout of laughter. The case was crammed: two pairs of spare shoes – both with heels – more tops than she could wear in twice their time away, and in the middle of it all, a hairdryer, a pair of straighteners and a big pink make-up box.

Amy picked up the hairdryer and cleared her laughter with a cough. 'Have you been camping before, Mia?'

'Yes. With my mum and my uncle. But the campsite where they go has fixed driers in the shower room and they're terrible for my hair. You can fit this one to a shaver socket – my mum gave me an adapter.'

Amy's dad took the hairdryer and in the kindest tone, he said, 'Where we are going, there aren't going to be any shaver sockets.' He placed it back in the case. 'And there won't be a shower room.'

Mia's brow creased. 'You sure? I thought all campsites have shower rooms.'

'I'll go and get the spare backpack,' he said. 'Then I'll show you how to pack for a real camping trip. You do have a hat, don't you – a cap or something?'

'Yeah. It's there.' She pulled out a purple baseball cap. It had sequins right across the peak.

'Good,' he said. 'Tie your hair back and put it on.'

Mia did so.

He picked up the hairdryer and straighteners. 'Now your hair is fixed, you don't need either of these.'

Bit by bit, they cut Mia's case right down to the essentials. They threw the packs into the back of the Land Rover, which stood on the driveway in stark contrast to her mum's car. Where that was spotless, cleaned on a weekly basis, the Land Rover belonged to her dad. It was splattered with mud and cleaned only when the rain came down.

Amy called over to Mia. 'Here, put these in too.'

Mia turned just in time to catch a huge coil of climbing rope. The expression on her face was a picture.

When they finally reached the Lake District, they pulled off the road on to what looked like a forgotten farmer's track. The Land Rover lurched this way and that, throwing them left and right with every bump and dip of the trail. Fifteen minutes later, Amy's dad parked.

Mia looked out through the side windows. 'Why are we stopping, Philip?'

Amy's dad opened his door. 'Because we're here. Out you get.'

Amy jumped out and pulled on her pack, taking a moment to get used to the shift in her centre of gravity. The pack was bulky, with a sleeping bag and ground mat rolled up and strapped to the bottom. She stepped from foot to foot, looking at Mia. 'Are you going to try yours on?'

But Mia was standing on the grass looking around. 'There's no campsite. Where are the tents?' Then a little higher. 'Where are our tents?'

'I've got them,' said Philip. 'Don't worry.'

'You mean we're camping here?'

'Nope.' He hitched his own pack up on his shoulders and pointed to the side of the mountain. 'Up there.'

It was a long, slow hike, during which Mia's initial shock soon changed to wonder and excitement. Tents that would fit several times inside a normal two-man tent were pitched under a heavy mist. After eating, they walked in the rain, and later, with light drizzle still coming down, they donned helmets, strapped each other into harnesses, and Mia, giggling like a child throughout, had her first experience of rock climbing and abseiling.

The memories brought a wave of sadness with them. As Amy looked up at the side of the house and prepared to climb, she wondered how her friend was coping.

She looked round to see Michelle watching her.

Maybe she should ask.

But right now, she was ready to climb.

They took a break for lunch in the kitchen. Michelle was standing at a gnarled, wooden table, removing the cling film from two large, plated salads. There was also a baguette stuffed with ham and cheese.

Salinger picked up the baguette without thanks and took a bite.

'We'll do two more hours, then call it a day.'

'More climbing?' asked Amy. 'Bring it on.'

Salinger took a second bite, and with his mouth stuffed, he shook his head. He chewed and swallowed hard in order to continue. 'We've done your body. Time to work on your brain.' He wiped the crumbs from his mouth. 'Have you done any electronics? You know, at school and stuff?'

'We did circuits in physics. Don't remember too much though.'

'I guess we're going to have to start from scratch then. When you're done eating, come and meet me in the library.'

Salinger left, taking his baguette with him, and Amy was left facing Michelle across table.

'Can I talk to her?' asked Amy. 'Mia. Can I talk to her? There must be a phone in the place you're keeping her.'

Michelle shook her head. 'Sorry. Mr Galloway's instructions were to keep you apart, and he was quite firm about it. When you know him like I do, you don't question. You just do. But once the job is complete, I'm very confident he'll relax. Believe me, the fact that he's moved her is a good sign. He's effectively removed the threat he had over you. Do you get that? From the way he talks about you, I'd say he's got a lot of faith in you.'

Amy looked behind her, at the open door. 'What about Jake? Does he think the same?'

'Why do you ask?'

Amy shrugged. 'I don't seem to get a lot back from him. He tells me to do stuff, I do it, then he tells me to do something else.'

'Does he tell you that you did it right?'

'Well he doesn't say I've done it wrong.'

Michelle's smile almost reached her eyes. 'What are you expecting? Applause? A pat on the back?' With a brief shake of her head she added, 'You'll be waiting a long time. I'm sure he'll let you know if you go wrong.'

'I get the same feeling. He's a bit of a slave-driver.'

'So I've seen.'

Amy waited until Michelle looked up before saying, 'Yeah. I noticed.'

* * *

In the library, a table had been cleared and had five different security devices set up on it. There were tools alongside: screwdrivers, miniature drivers, snips, pliers and multimeters.

Salinger skirted the table. 'Getting into the room is one thing. Getting the painting is another. It isn't just hanging on a hook up there. It's behind safety glass, and the safety glass is clamped with electromagnetic solenoids to metal casing that is sunk into the wall. So unless you can get a JCB up to the eighteenth, you'll need to be able to crack the security system. On the bright side, there are only a few security devices that fit the bill. I'm going to show you how to crack them all, so open your eyes, clear your ears, and get your brain in gear, because every second you're working on the real thing, you'll be wide open and vulnerable.'

By evening, Amy was physically exhausted, mentally exhilarated and emotionally distressed. She still felt bad about Mia, she still missed home, but there was so much other stuff buzzing around her head that she couldn't settle on anything long enough to worry. She just lay there, in a bed, in a house in the middle of nowhere, staring up at the ceiling with images of the day looking back at her.

Before falling asleep, the last thing that crossed her mind was a single thought.

At least Mia is safe.

Mia lay wide awake in the early morning hours. She had so much going on in her head that getting back to sleep was impossible. Thoughts ranged from her mum, and how she would be reacting to this, to other family members, and of course, Dan. Dan the Man. How long had he hung around the shopping centre waiting for Mia to show up? How would he feel if he knew where she was? Shocked? Sickened? Or did he watch the kind of stuff they filmed here? They say that all boys have a porn stash . . . No. She didn't even want to consider it.

She was also occupied with what was going on outside. It was probably the noise that had disturbed her in the first place. She had heard arguments, and young men yelling abuse as they passed by the houses. Then a car pulled up, its stereo so loud that she could hear the bass thumping all the way up here. There was a whole load of swearing and screaming. It sounded like a fight. The dogs in the back yard were going crazy while the same deep voice she'd heard before yelled at them to shut their noise. She heard the roar of an engine, the screech of wheel-spin, as the car shot off. And through it all, Scarlet slept soundly.

This affected Mia more than the noise. She lay on her side watching Scarlet, wondering what had been so bad in her life that this was considered safe. And how regular was the calamity outside for her to sleep this soundly? It was enough to drive anyone insane, but considering what else had been going through her mind, Mia was grateful for the distraction.

Perhaps if she got up out of bed and could see what was going on, it might not seem so frightening.

At the window, she couldn't see anything other than the back yard. From the sound of things, the action was going on at the front of the house. It sounded like the same car was back. There was a load of laughter and more abuse.

Seconds later, Mia heard the unmistakable gravelly voice of Marge screaming at them, throwing just as much abuse back.

Maybe that's why Scarlet felt so secure. She had Marge down there keeping the scum at bay. From what Mia had seen of her so far, Marge certainly didn't seem the type to take stuff like that lying down.

A moment later, she heard Marge cry out, 'Ed! Get the dogs out here.'

And with that came something she could see. Down below, in the back yard, a man, bulging at the seams with muscle appeared with two dogs on chains. They were of the same breed. What had Scarlet called them? Canary Mastiffs? Whatever they were, they looked deadly.

The man holding their chains was goading them. 'You gonna get 'em boys? Yeah? Gonna get 'em? Sick 'em?'

The dogs were fired up, jumping and barking like crazy while the man unlocked the back gate.

A car horn blared out, and together with the laughter of young men, it almost drowned Marge's yells of, 'Ed!'

Down below, 'On my way.' The padlock was off the gates. Ed unhooked the catch and the two dogs almost dragged him out.

The gate was left open.

Mia blinked, hardly able to believe what she was seeing. The gate was open. The dogs were gone. She was looking down at the way out!

She didn't waste any more time. She grabbed her jeans, pulled them on, slipped her feet into her trainers and, as gently as she could, she lifted the window.

With the window open, the noise out there was so much louder, and behind her, Scarlet gave a low moan. It was enough to make Mia freeze.

Scarlet twisted on her bed, turned over and muttered something. The noise had disturbed her, but for now, she was still asleep, or not awake enough to realise something was going on. Mia couldn't take the chance of that happening. If Scarlet *did* wake up, and she saw her, she'd either try to stop her once more, or worse – she'd call out.

Mia turned away and slipped out of the window.

She was balanced on the ledge, on the second floor of an old Victorian terrace. The bricks were ancient, but unlike modern buildings, where every brick is flush and details are few, the outside of this place was littered with hand and footholds. Difficulty wise, it was a walk in the park compared to the climbs Amy and her dad had put Mia through. It was also a fraction of the distance – there was a small brick outhouse just a few metres away.

As she worked her way along, she took care to keep her head down and hurried as she passed the next window along. The curtains were drawn, but she couldn't risk the idea that someone would decide to look out, to see what all the noise was about, just as Mia was standing there.

In just a few seconds, she was close enough to make the leap to the roof of the outhouse. She turned and pushed herself into the air, taking the impact of the landing with a tight crouch. The only sound was a light thump – nothing compared to the noise and chaos going on in the front street. It sounded like those dogs were in a frenzy.

She took a quick look around. Every wall in every back yard in the whole terrace was topped with broken glass set in cement and topped off with barbed wire. The only way forward was to drop down into the yard.

Mia squatted, turned and dropped down. The dogs were gone, the gates were still open . . .

. . . and so was the back door.

A woman was standing there, looking directly at Mia.

Mia's heart skipped a beat, but the woman just stood there, watching. Her eyes were only half open, she seemed to sway on her feet as she took a drag on a long, rolled joint and gave a weak, 'Hey,' clearly stoned out of her brains.

Mia straightened, stepped backwards towards the gate, then turned and ran.

Out the front, the dogs were still barking, but they sounded further away. Mia guessed the man holding their chains had either let them go, or was giving chase.

She headed the other way, ran past wheelie bins and broken bottles until she reached the end of the back lane. To her right she could see the main street – the last place she wanted to be. To the left was another back lane. She had no idea where it led, but who cared? It led away from here, and that was the main thing.

Mia ran.

SCARLET'S ROOM
NO. 12

'Scarlet!'

Scarlet stirred and turned to see Marge looming over her, fury cut into every crease on her old, weathered face. She managed a groan and something like, 'What . . . ?'

'Wake up and take a look, is *what*,' croaked Marge. The stench of cigarettes and bad breath was putrid, enough to cause Scarlet to shift back on her bed as she looked about the room.

'What's going on?'

'Where is she?' demanded Marge. 'Where's the girl?'

Scarlet sat up. She noticed the open window, the empty bed, the duvet cast aside and no sign of Mia.

'Oh, no.' It was still dark outside. She could hear the dogs downstairs, Ed shouting at them, and all kinds of calamity out in the hall. 'When did this happen?'

'Well I'm guessing it happened while you were sound asleep.'

Scarlet was on her feet, holding her arms out to keep some space between Marge and herself while she snapped back, 'Now wait a second. You told me I had a room-mate for a few days. No one said a thing about being that girl's jailer. If she's so important, why isn't she locked up?'

'She is, you stupid bitch. Or she was.'

Scarlet was at the window, looking down at the back yard, cringing at the thought of what those animals could have done to a fifteen-year-old girl. 'I can't believe she took the risk, not after I told her about the dogs.' Then she looked at Marge. 'How did she get past the dogs? She did, didn't she?'

For the first time, Marge actually looked nervous, and dropped her gaze.

Scarlet realised she was onto something. 'What? What aren't you telling me?'

Marge's eyes flicked to the window and back, then she seemed to deflate a touch as she said, 'The dogs weren't there. They were out the front, with Ed.'

Scarlet just looked at her. Before she could say anything else, Marge raised her voice and added. 'We had a situation. I'm surprised you didn't hear it yourself.'

'I can remember some shouting – we get that most weekends.'

'So you just turned over and went back to sleep while she,' Marge stuck a thumb towards the empty bed, 'climbed out of the window?'

'And walked past the security *you* removed?' Scarlet smiled, realising she was winning this match 'I'm guessing you even left the gate open to save her a climb.'

Marge looked ready to burst, but Scarlet just shook

her head. 'Unbelievable. I'd hate to be the one to have to explain –'

Marge's hand shot out, grabbing Scarlet by the throat. Scarlet struggled and tried to pull away, but Marge was strong. Her hands were fat with a grip like a wrestler and held Scarlet firm as she put her mouth right up to her face. 'You talk to me like that again, and a few marks will be the last of your worries. You got me?'

She thrust Scarlet back on the bed, but rather than looking victorious, she looked very, very worried as she glanced back down at the empty bed. She appeared to make a decision, her confidence returning as she snapped, 'I want everyone out looking for her. I want her found before dawn, because if I have to make that call, I swear, we'll all be for the chop.'

BACK LANES
UNKNOWN TOWN

Mia ran blind through back lanes, making sure that every time she took a left, she balanced it out with a right somewhere further along. Even when she thought she was far enough away to step out on to the main streets, they all looked so identical that she got locked in paranoia that she was going full circle.

Her priority was finding somewhere safe – ideally, the nearest police station, but her initial surge of adrenalin was wavering, she was dragging tiredness, exhaustion and fear like a dead weight behind her. Her body was screaming out at her to stop, but she refused to give in, pushing and pushing on with everything she had left.

She reached what looked like a main road. The houses here were larger, set back from the pavement by gardens and driveways and the grass verge was lined with trees. She continued for some distance before reaching a roundabout and a sign that read, 'TOWN CENTRE' *Which town?* She wanted to scream, before she realised that the sign pointed back down a road almost parallel to the road she'd come along.

She took a moment to collect her thoughts, to calm her growing panic and reassure herself that although it seemed she was backtracking a little, at least now she knew she was going the right way.

The sky was lightening. Mia had no idea of the time, possibly 5am, maybe even earlier. It was certainly not much later. Her main worry was that as time went on, she would be more and more visible.

Okay, so maybe if she kept to the side streets – even just one block of houses away from that main road, she could keep out of sight. If anyone from the terrace was after her, they'd be in a car. At the moment, it was probably too late for taxis taking people home, too early for buses taking people to work. She was in that dead zone between, so if she did see headlights, all she had to do was hide.

Okay. So that was the plan. Go!

She passed a newsagent – closed and locked up with metal shutters. She paused for a moment, wondering what time these places opened. It must be early. In fact, it must be around now, it must be . . .

Unless it was shut down, out of business.

Forget it. In the town centre there would be a police station, and every step she took was one step closer.

Mia pushed on.

She knew she was getting closer. There were fewer houses, more shops. All shut – most with shutters or cages locked down. A car approached, and Mia ducked into a doorway, slipping on a discarded kebab. She let the car go past, scraped her foot clean and kept going.

Five minutes later, with the streetlights still on, but the sky becoming worryingly light, she got to a point where the road turned sharply to the right. Ahead, a pedestrianised shopping area stretched out between so many familiar names. And right on the corner, a signpost with three branches, each pointing in different directions: POLICE STATION, BUS STATION, TRAIN STATION. Mia picked up her stride and followed the road to the right.

And then she saw something that caused her to stop dead and take a sharp sidestep into a doorway.

She stood there a moment, hardly able to catch her breath through fear, then she peered out and looked again at what she thought she had seen.

Up ahead was a small town centre police station. It was an old brick building with steps, as well as a ramp at the side for wheelchairs, leading up to two large blue doors with square glass panels. But what had made Mia stop in her tracks was the man leaning on the railings at the foot of the steps. He was drinking from a polystyrene cup and looking thoroughly fed up.

There were a thousand different reasons for anyone to be standing right there but no matter how many she came up with, none shook the real fear that he was keeping watch, that he was waiting for her.

It wasn't such a coincidence, was it? If *you* were kidnapped, and you had managed to escape, where would you go?

Should she wait? Hang around until a police officer came out?

It certainly seemed like a good idea, but every moment

that she was waiting here meant she was visible to any cars that came this way. And if one of those cars happened to have someone who definitely was looking for her, she was a sitting duck. So no, waiting was not an option.

Okay, think. If the police station was out of bounds – at least for now – where else could she go?

It was Monday morning. Getting on for half five, maybe 6am. Too early to hide in a crowd. Too early to shout and scream and make a scene, and too risky to approach anyone on their own. The place was completely dead. Why would it be anything else? The people with jobs would only just be leaving home . . .

And then it hit her. The bus station. The shops were shut, but there would be a whole load of people on their way to open up, to check stock and get ready for the day. And where would they land? The bus station. There'd be someone with a phone. She could even go straight to one of the drivers, get *him* to make a call.

That was that. Decision made. She backtracked to the signpost and ran across the designer cobbles of the market square. She passed another sign for the bus station pointing straight ahead. The pathway led under a bridge, and she could see steps on the other side.

A quick look over her shoulder reassured Mia that she wasn't being followed, then she entered the underpass. Tired, dizzy and feeling sick from exhaustion and fear, she pushed on.

She didn't see the two figures melt from out of the shadows, but she heard the voice . . .

'You going somewhere, little girl?'

Galloway was furious. He very rarely went to the terrace. It was a part of his empire that he liked to keep at arm's length. It was something that ticked along nicely on its own, earning a steady income without him ever having to make his presence known. If they thought he was angry on the phone, it was nothing compared to what he was going to say when he got there in person.

He had his seatbelt off and was opening the car door as the car slowed to a stop. He kept his face down and marched quickly and directly to number 12.

Marge was standing there, and from the look on her face, he guessed she had a whole load of things prepared. He didn't even give her a chance to get started.

'Inside,' he ordered.

She held up a hand, 'Can I just say –'

'I said, inside.'

He pushed past, wanting to be off the street and out of public view as soon as possible. Once inside the hallway, he turned and bellowed, 'You told me this place was secure. You assured me she would be contained.'

Marge's face was fixed with a grim determination to get her own words out in defence. 'Under normal circumstances . . .'

'These are *not* normal circumstances, something which I am sure I made perfectly clear when I first told you about this girl.'

'This terrace is not a prison, Mr Galloway, but for the likes of a young girl, I thought having security on the front door would be more than enough.'

'So tell me again, how did she get out? No, in fact, hold that. I want you to show me, take me through events step by step because I can't actually *believe* what I'm hearing.' There was an edge to his tone that put pause to Marge's response. She took a moment to compose herself.

'We had a bit of an incident last night,' she explained. 'It's not a regular thing, but every now and then a bunch of lads come down here and give the girls a hard time.'

Galloway tightened his lips.

Marge didn't hold back. 'What do you expect us to do? Let them have their fun, scare off the few customers the girls have? Because that's what they do. And with no customers, we've got no income. No money, Mr Galloway, and I've had it up to here. Last night they went one step too far. The last thing on my mind was babysitting some little girl.'

Galloway stepped forward, enough to pin Marge against the stair banister. 'When you take explicit instructions from me, it should have been the *only* thing on your mind. She is *not* just some little girl. I made it clear. Clear! She was to be kept safe. But you couldn't hold her for two nights!'

Marge held up a hand and shouted him down. 'I've got people looking for her. They went out first thing, as soon as we realised she was gone. I sent a whole team to find her, and I gave them strict instructions not to return empty handed.' She calmed her voice down a touch. 'We've a good idea where she'll go. It's just a case of cutting her off and waiting.'

'Just a case of cutting her off? That simple, eh?' Galloway checked his watch. 'Well she's had a bloody good head start. What if she gets to the police? It won't take them long to realise who she is. The first thing they're going to do is listen to what she's got to say very, very carefully, and from that, they'll have a pretty good idea where she's been for the past day and a half. It isn't going to take them long to turn up here asking questions.'

Marge folded her arms, an image of defiant confidence. 'Police don't bother us. They know we do a service. My girls are clean, professional and a damn sight safer here than out on the streets.'

'But we're not talking about *your* girls, and we're not talking about a small, local case of a back-street brothel. We're talking about a nationwide appeal to find two kidnapped teenage girls. If she is picked up, then in a few hours, the whole country is going to be focussed on *this* terrace. *This* street is going to be crawling with journalists, news teams, photographers, not to mention every nosy local who wants to get in on the action.' He slammed his hand against the banister. 'I can't *believe* this.'

Marge shouted over him, 'If you let me finish! The first thing I did was send someone to keep an eye on the police station, and he's still there now, soon to be joined by a few more.'

'Too little too late,' yelled back Galloway. He glanced about. 'I want the whole place cleared. This house first, starting with the film equipment, cameras, computers, the lot. Get it out and stored somewhere. I want no evidence at all of what's been going on here. Spread the word that there's going to be a big police presence at any moment. Blame it on the fight last night if that makes it any easier, just get the word out and get everyone you can out of the way until this blows over. The local press will have their day, sell a few copies with pictures of front doors, but if there's no one to photograph, no one to arrest and no one to question, we're one step ahead.'

Marge's skin went a touch paler. 'So . . . So, you're closing us down? Is that it?'

Galloway looked her directly in the eye. 'You got a better idea?'

Mia froze.

The two lads had a relaxed swagger as they stepped into view, splitting up, moving to either side, laughing. Their arms were held out as though to indicate they meant no harm, but their hands looked ready to grab. Both were dishevelled, both were a fair bit older than Mia. The first had short, messy hair, the other, had long, dirty blond dreadlocks. There was a strong smell of BO and stale alcohol about the two of them.

'Hey, I'm talking to you,' said dreadlocks. 'You going somewhere?'

He was tall and walked towards her, arms stretched wide, enough to tell her she was being closed in.

The other skirted behind her. Mia winced at the sound of his laughter – high-pitched, bordering on insanity.

'I'm not going back,' she said. 'And if you try . . .'

'Not going back where, sweetheart?' Dreadlocks was grinning inanely, showing two missing teeth.

The penny dropped. They were nothing to do with the terrace – but they were in her way, holding her up.

She pushed her fear aside and glared at the young man in front of her. 'Get away from me.'

'What's wrong, love? We just want to chat? Don't you want to chat with us?' His smile faded. 'You think we're scum, is that it?'

'I just want to get past.'

'You too good for us, is *that* it?' He looked to his mate. 'Students, eh? We welcome them to our home town and how do they treat us?'

Arms grabbed Mia from behind. She tried to turn, but he was strong and held her tight. She tried stamping back, but he was keeping his legs wide and continued to laugh manically in her ear.

Dreadlocks stepped forward and grabbed her by the shoulder. 'We're the trolls that live under the bridge, love. You want to get past us, you've got to pay up.'

'Got to pay!' repeated the idiot behind her.

'I haven't got anything,' hissed Mia. Again she tried to twist, but she could feel her strength was ebbing. How much longer could she keep this up? How much was too much. Wouldn't it be easier just to give up?

Dreadlocks pushed his face closer. His stubble was as filthy as his dreads, and his lips were dry and chapped. 'Oh, we think you've got more than you realise.'

She tried again to fight, but her attempt to strike with her knee was weak and badly timed. Dreadlocks simply moved aside, taking the impact on the outside of his leg.

'Naughty, naughty,' he said, a smile back on his face.

'Oh, she's a naughty one,' giggled the other.

THUMP.

Dreadlocks' eyes bulged wide in a moment of utter surprise before he slumped forward, straight into Mia.

The one behind called out, 'Danny?'

His name took Mia by surprise. Danny. Dan. The same name as . . .

But Danny was down, and Mia's thoughts were cut dead by the figure standing behind him – the monstrous figure that had been holding the dogs' chains last night, the one Marge had screamed at. Ed.

Up close, he was uglier than she'd imagined. Spots, stubble and a scar running down the side of his face.

Danny had barely hit the ground when Ed's arm shot out. Mia tensed, convinced that he was going to punch her right in the face. Instead, his open hand reached right past her and grabbed the other young man, the one standing behind her, who screamed high and wild, and Mia was instantly released.

Ed took hold of her wrist – not too tight, but firm enough that she was never going to pull free and spoke directly to her. 'Maybe now you'll understand why Marge likes to keep her girls safe.' He pulled the other lad round, gripping him firmly by the back of the neck. 'She doesn't like the scum on the street getting their filthy paws on you.'

Ed squeezed, taking visible pleasure as the lad in his grip began to yell in pain.

Mia took the chance to try and pull free, but Ed just smiled and shook his head. 'Sorry, trouble. But you're coming with me. And you,' he twisted the lad by his neck so he was facing him. 'You are going to get lost.'

With a hefty push, he knocked the lad down on to Dreadlocks. Without giving them any more attention, he pulled a mobile from his pocket.

'Yeah, Marge? It's Ed.' A short pause. 'Oh, yeah, I've got her all right. I'm bringing her back now.'

As he shut the phone, Mia felt like she was going to collapse. She couldn't fight any more. She didn't have the strength. Her only option was the utter futility of pleading, crying, of hoping he'd see sense.

'No!' Her struggles were weak as she desperately tried to think again of what Amy would do. She thought of the van, of Amy's advice to kick and scream and make a scene.

Other than the two scuffs currently getting to their feet, the underpass was deserted. But she had to try. She had to give one last fight.

But when she twisted, he held her firm. When she tried to scream, nothing more than a croak escaped her lips.

Ed's hand clapped firmly over her mouth and nose, and his voice was in her ear. 'You've caused us enough bother. You keep doing that, and I'm going to . . .'

CRACK.

The noise was sickening. Ed's eyes seemed to glaze over, his grip on Mia relaxed and he dropped, first to his knees, then face forward to the ground. Spots of blood, clearly visible through his short, blond skinhead, welled up.

Behind him, standing in a slight stoop, with a grimace on his face and half a house brick gripped in his hand, stood the scruffy, dreadlocked figure of Danny.

BEDROOM
WEST HALL MANOR

Amy's eyes flicked open. Light was fighting its way in through the curtains, but the clock on the wall reassured her that it was still early. She rolled from her side on to her back and once again, was staring up at the ceiling. This time, the only thing looking back at her was the plain, white ceiling.

She wondered how long it would be until she was back outside, training once more. She was no stranger to prolonged exercise, but there was a definite ache in her limbs – not painful, and not particularly uncomfortable, just a small, physical reminder of the work she'd put in.

She felt a wave of satisfaction as she stretched and slowly turned onto her other side, adjusting her head to snuggle a little deeper into the double, goose-down pillows.

Despite the worries that should be bearing down on her, she couldn't ignore a growing thrill at the thought of what she was doing, of what she was training to be. She really was going to do something that no one else could. And it wasn't only the athletic side that thrilled her. She couldn't believe she'd got to grips with electronic circuits so easily, following the path of the switch wires, tracing them to their source to determine which to cut, getting it right time after time. Salinger had been so cool when he tried to show her how fast she should be able to crack those circuits. He didn't seem quite so cool when she finally beat his time. He'd only growled something about care versus speed.

But despite the satisfaction, Amy didn't get completely lost in fantasy as she lay there. There was a single thought that kept her firmly in touch with reality, and the reason she was really doing this.

Mia.

Mia stood facing Danny. He still had the half-brick in his hand and was glaring down at the crumpled figure on the ground. The sound of the crack that had knocked him to the floor had just as effectively hit the wind out of Mia. A second ago, she was pulling away from that monster, ready to run. Right now, she could only stare as the blood on his head began to run down the curve of his head.

She felt overcome with weakness. Enough was enough. There was no point in running. If these two could do that to a muscled steroid monster, there was no way she was going to escape. Might as well stay here a while, especially when her legs were jelly and her head kept telling her, you're just too tired . . . far too tired.

Danny spoke to the other lad. 'You okay, Martin?'

The one who had been so full of giggles, and now so quiet, was on his feet. 'Yeah. Jesus, that's Eddie Flynn. I thought he was going to strangle me for real.'

'And what about you?' said Danny.

It took a moment for Mia to realise he was talking

to her, asking how she was. She didn't know how to respond. Words wouldn't come.

'Hey!'

She looked up, Danny was looking right at her. 'What have you done to get him after you? You ripped him off or something?'

Mia managed a slight shake of the head.

'Whatever,' said Danny. 'We best get going before he gets up.' He waved a hand in front of Mia's face. 'You okay? Hey! He's not dead, if that's what you're thinking. But he's going to have a hell of a headache when he comes round.'

He reached for her hand. Mia instinctively pulled away.

'Hey,' repeated Danny, his tone a little softer. 'It's okay. We were just mucking around. Thought you were a student from the university. Sometimes we wind them up. Nothing serious, like. We just give them a bit of a time, give them a bit of abuse and they give it back, call us scum. Just a bit of banter really.'

Banter? Mia thought. Five minutes ago, she thought they were going to kill her.

'I'm not a student.'

'Yeah, I kind of guessed that when he turned up. But whatever you are, love, you need to get going. If he wakes up, he'll murder us all.'

Mia just stared down at the man on the ground. 'He wants to take me back.'

There was a groan and Ed moved his head to one side, began to move an arm.

Danny grabbed Mia by the hand. This time, Mia didn't have time to pull away.

'What are you doing, man?' asked Martin.

'She's coming with us.'

'What the hell for?'

'Because she's lost the plot. Just look at her.'

The man on the ground gave a sudden, almighty roar. He twisted round, flailing with his right arm, missing Mia's leg by millimetres.

Martin cried out, jumping back.

Danny held Mia's hand tighter and yanked her away from Ed. 'Run.'

Mia staggered two steps, but held back, looking at the man on the ground, none of this making any sense.

Ed began to push himself up.

Danny yelled, 'Come *on!*' He yanked her again, putting his other hand on her back to keep her moving.

As Eddie Flynn struggled to his feet, the three of them legged it through the underpass, back into the bright morning light and back towards the centre of town.

Mia looked back. Ed had slumped back to his knees and was holding the back of his head with one hand, using the other to steady himself. He was glaring at them like a man possessed, and trying once again to get back on his feet.

'This way,' cried Danny. He pulled Mia towards a lane that cut through the back of shops. The buildings here were high, and the lane was narrow and clogged with junk and litter and massive green dumpsters. What looked like a dead end was in fact a right turn where they had to jump over a pile of refuse and rotting waste.

Panic began to catch up with Mia. She tried to slow down, shouting as she was pulled along, 'Where are you taking me? Let me go. Please, just let me go.'

But Danny didn't listen. He gripped her hand tighter and ordered her to keep going. They changed direction, ran out into the light of another deserted street, then cut across to the opposite back lane where they pulled into the alcove of a doorway with a messy, hand-painted sign that read 'KEEP CLEAR!'

Danny put his finger to his lips. 'Ssh.' He peered and looked back along the lane, towards the open street. He kept his voice low. 'No sign of him so far.'

'We'll hear him long before we see him,' said Martin.

Danny released his grip on Mia and asked, 'Are you okay?'

But Mia was still wary, still confused. How could they switch so easily? One minute they were threatening her, the next, saving. Somehow, she felt a second wind of energy and a renewed desire to escape. She pulled away from Danny and replied, 'Why? What are you planning to do to me?'

'I told you, we were just mucking around. I never thought for a second you'd have someone like him after you.'

Martin looked out too, pulling straight back in, still catching his breath. 'What did you mean when you said he wants to take you back?'

'I don't know.' Mia lay back against the wall. Should she tell them? Would it make any difference if she did? She slowly shook her head and said, 'Some house. I was kind of kidnapped.'

'Kidnapped?' Danny looked suspicious, but Mia couldn't be bothered with explanation.

She closed her eyes for a moment and released a nervous laugh. 'So what now? You going to drag me to where you two live?' She gave a shrug like she didn't really care. 'Can't be much worse than where I was.'

'This is where we live,' said Martin.

Mia looked about at the filthy back lane.

'Yeah,' said Danny with a lopsided grin. 'Sorry the place is a bit of a mess, love. We weren't expecting company.'

'Yeah, right.' Mia closed her eyes once more. She couldn't be bothered with games or jokes or whatever these two were up to. Right now, she was trying to get her mind back on track, to focus on how to get away, and where to go next. The police station was guarded, and now that she'd been seen trying to get to the bus station, she guessed that was out too.

'Anything?' asked Martin, and straight after, Danny replied, 'Nothing.'

Mia guessed they were still looking out for Ed. She took a deep breath, her heart rate finally calming down.

She heard Martin slouch against the wall next to her. Her nose wrinkled. Strange, during the fear and the flight, she'd hardly noticed just how pungent the body odour on these boys was. She opened her eyes and looked again, first at Martin, then Danny. Both were filthy, both had several days' stubble. Their clothes were layered, shirts over T-shirts over T-shirts, and their jeans looked like they'd never been cleaned – ever.

'You telling me you're homeless?'

Danny nodded. 'For now. We're busy looking for another squat. We had some trouble at our last place.'

'Where you really kidnapped?' said Martin. 'Like, for real? By Eddie Flynn?'

Mia took a moment to decide whether or not they were still playing games. If the story of her and Amy was in the paper, then it had probably been on the TV too. A kidnap, a triple murder and a house blowing up: that was big-time stuff. But maybe if they really were homeless, they didn't watch too much TV.

'It complicated,' she said, too tired to even try.

'So where are you going now?'

Mia shrugged. 'I was heading for the bus station. Thought I'd find help. I tried the police first, but couldn't get anywhere near.'

'Why not?'

'Because there was some bloke standing guard, waiting for me to show up.'

Danny looked at Martin. Something seemed to pass between them, then Martin shrugged and nodded. 'Nothing else to do.'

Mia felt her stomach tighten. 'What?'

'Days on the street are pretty dull,' said Danny. He pushed himself to his feet. 'Especially mornings. He interlocked his fingers, bending them outwards with a crack. 'But now . . . now we've got a challenge.'

***

Danny and Martin led Mia through more back streets then paused at a corner. Danny held up a hand and carefully peered out.

'Is that him?'

Mia crept up behind him and took a quick look. The guy who had been leaning on the handrails had moved. He was now standing at the corner of the building. He was talking on a mobile and looking the other way.

'Yeah, that's him.' She was about to step back into the alley when she noticed another figure standing at the railings, guarding the entrance to the police station. A young woman, slim, wearing a long leather coat. And she had bright-red hair.

Scarlet.

Mia pulled back and pressed herself hard against the wall. She could hardly believe what she'd seen.

'What's up?'

Mia took another glance. 'She's one too. The girl.'

Danny looked out. 'If they've got two out there, there might be more.' He glanced at Martin. 'You want to check it out?'

Martin nodded, sniffed, and walked out.

Mia pulled back further into alley. 'What's he doing?'

'Just hang fire, girl. We need to know what we're up against if we're going to help you out.'

Five minutes later, Martin returned via the back alley.

'Well, I hate to tell you this,' he said, 'but it looks likes there are a few more. And Eddie Flynn's one of them.'

'Did he see you?'

'Nah. We're pretty much invisible at the best of times, but I made sure to keep out of view. He's right round the other side, probably thinks you're going to take the long way round. There are two more on the main street and a parked car. And there's a driver in the car. Looks like they *really* want you back. Anyway, on my travels . . .' He held up the front page of a crumpled newspaper. 'I got this.'

Danny frowned for a second, then uttered, 'Woah! That's her,' then to Mia, 'That's you.'

Mia looked. It was yesterday's – a Sunday newspaper – and her story was stretched down the right-hand side

'Oh my god.'

She grabbed the paper, looking first at the two main photographs, one of herself, the other of Amy. The photographs were similar size, but the one of Amy had been cropped, making her face more prominent. There was a third photograph, showing the remains of the house.

'I guess she was telling the truth,' said Martin.

Mia barely heard him. She was scanning the article, skipping over details about Amy, hailed as a world-class gymnast, hunting for information about home. How was her family coping? Did they know she was alive? But the article ended prematurely. It gave the basic details of the kidnap, the condition of the house on Ashdale Crescent and ended with a link to the main story.

'Where's the rest of the paper?' she asked.

'That's all there was,' replied Martin. 'Sorry.'

Danny gave the main street another look. 'There's no way you'll get to the police station. Making a run for it is out.'

'Why?' asked Mia.

'Because they're expecting you, and they've got their distraction in place. That's what the girl is for. As soon as you appear, they'll move fast. And while you're being whipped away, the girl will scream like crazy, pretending she's been mugged or beaten up – anything it takes to draw the attention away from you.'

'But this should make things a little less tricky,' said Martin, holding up the paper.

Danny shook his head. 'They'll never believe us. They'll think it's just another wind-up.'

'What I mean is, if we can't get her to the police, why don't we bring the police here, then we show them the paper, and then they'll see the girl.'

'I thought you said they wouldn't believe you,' said Mia.

Danny gave Martin a nod of agreement, then he said to Mia, 'They won't. But if we go in there and shout "All coppers are wankers", they usually give chase. If we swipe something, it'll give them extra incentive.'

'You're kidding.' She looked from one to the other. 'Aren't you?'

'Usually we do this for kicks,' said Martin. 'But today, we're on a legitimate errand. So stay right here, kidnap girl; we'll be back in a mo.'

LIMOUSINE
OUTSKIRTS OF TOWN

Galloway had his left elbow against the passenger window of the car. His hand was slowly pushing back through his hair. His eyes were wide with tension, as he focused on the road ahead. Something on the radio broke his line of thought. His hand shot out and silenced the radio with a thump.

The driver noticed, then gave Galloway a quick glance. 'Radiohead don't do it for you, eh?'

'I've had enough surprises for one day, Mack. Now is not the time for jokes.' He pulled out his mobile and hit the contacts. A moment later, it was ringing.

Michelle's voice came on the line almost immediately.

'Mr Galloway? Is everything all right?'

Galloway got straight to the point. 'No, Michelle. Everything is far from being all right. Where's the girl?'

'Amy? She's hanging by a rope, halfway up the side of the house. She's working with Jake. Looks like they're getting along.'

Galloway actually sighed. Considering his day so far,

he was surprised to find the walls were still standing. 'Has she been near the gates at all?'

'No,' replied Michelle. 'She's been working all day.'

'So she hasn't tried the code?'

'She hasn't been out of my sight.'

The answer didn't alleviate his concern. 'You did give her a false code, didn't you?'

'Of course.'

'Right, well, let's keep psychology to one side from here on in. I want to avoid any risks and keep to something tried and tested. Line of sight. Got that? Keep her in view at all times. I do not want that girl to be anywhere, not for a moment, without yourself or Jake Salinger knowing exactly where she is.'

'I've been watching her all morning, Mr Galloway. From what I've seen, they seem to be making good progress. She certainly appears motivated enough to take things seriously.'

'Good. Hold on.' He put the mobile aside. 'Keep the speed down, will you, Mack?'

'Sorry, boss. Just trying to get you back like you said: as quick as I can.'

'Yeah, well scratch that and get me back as *safely* as you can: i.e. don't give our boys in blue any excuse to come after us. Unmarked cars everywhere these days. I don't think I can take any more bad news.'

'You got it.'

Galloway put the phone back to his ear. 'Okay, Michelle, I'm back.'

'You sound uneasy. Are there problems?'

'You could say that, Michelle, if you consider the other girl doing a runner a problem. So, yes, right now, I do feel a tad uneasy.'

'What?' The alarm was clear in Michelle's voice. 'How on earth did she –'

'Don't ask me how, just make sure Amy May does not find out. Keep her away from televisions. Cut the satellite feed. Radios too. Have them removed if you have to, but make sure there is no access to any news channels whatsoever. Make up some lie, or better still, keep her so busy she won't have time to think about it.'

'I thought the terrace was supposed to be secure.'

Galloway shouted her down. 'I'd appreciate it if you keep that information strictly to yourself, Michelle. I don't want any risk of this being overheard. Do you understand me?'

'It's okay, they're a good distance away. They're outside. I'm in the lounge, next to the bar.'

'Doing what?'

'Having a break. I am allowed. Don't panic, Mr Galloway. Amy is still in my line of sight, but far enough away that I'm not nursing her.'

Galloway pulled the phone from his ear a moment, gritted his teeth, then he pressed it back to his face and growled, 'I don't care how far away she is, Michelle. To say this is sensitive is putting it mildly, so keep your lips sealed. I want Amy May to think we have all the cards in our hands. If she even *suspects* that her friend is out of the equation, we're going to be in a very difficult position.'

'I understand perfectly, Mr Galloway.'

'Good. I'll talk to Jake too. I need to speed things up a bit, get this operation under way tomorrow if possible, before the plod comes knocking. Time is against us on this one, so I'm putting things in order now. As far as Amy is concerned, if they stop for a rest, keep her busy, keep her occupied. I've got a few other things to sort, but I should be there late afternoon. By which time, I might have calmed down enough to hold a conversation with the girl. As for tonight . . .'

He only paused for a second, but Michelle was quick to jump in. 'I'll tell her she needs time to contemplate things, keep herself focused.'

She was trying to help. That was good, and Galloway was finally beginning to calm down, but it wasn't quite what he had in mind. 'I was actually thinking of stretching the evening out in a more relaxed way,' he said. 'Tell Alice to prepare something nice. We'll eat in the main dining room. Just you, myself and Amy. I want to continue that feeling of what's on offer, make her feel special, because I want the rest of this plan to go like clockwork.' He took a breath, and in a slightly calmer voice, he said, 'I don't just want Amy May to do this job, Michelle. I want her to *want* to do it.'

GARDEN
WEST HALL MANOR

Around midday, Amy stood on the lawn at the back of the house. Salinger lay a black canvas bag gently on the ground.

'Well, your climbing is fast and pretty much flawless,' said Salinger. 'And you can abseil like a pro. But now you get to try something you're not so familiar with. Scaling distance on a wire.'

He opened the bag to reveal multiple parts of a device, each strapped into place. Amy thought she could recognise several of these parts immediately: a stock, a trigger, a telescopic sight.

'Some kind of rifle?'

Jake shook his head. 'It's a grappling hook. And here's the rope.' He dropped a large coil of thin, black rope on the ground. 'Ultra lightweight, but very, very strong. Certainly strong enough for a girl of your size.'

As he spoke, he began taking parts out and clicking them together.

'Shouldn't I be doing that?'

'Not necessary,' replied Salinger. 'I'm going to be up

there with you to fire it, and I'll be watching you every step of the way.'

Amy didn't give up. 'You said I'd earned the right to be your apprentice.' She reached out a hand. 'So show me.'

Salinger paused for a moment, looking at her. He glanced at the house, then back to Amy. Finally, he nodded. 'Fair enough. Here you go.'

Amy took the parts, and following Jake's step-by-step instructions, she assembled the rest.

'This is what makes it fire,' said Salinger. He handed her a large black cylinder. 'This is compressed air. No flash and not much noise. It screws in here, see?'

Amy nodded and fitted the cylinder in place.

'Okay, you've got your hardware ready, but before we do anything else, you need to tether one end of your wire. Do that now: tether the bottom of the coil, so it feeds from the top. The less resistance you have, the more accurate your shot.'

Again, Amy followed instructions carefully. Salinger watched but his only acknowledgement that she had done it right was a brief nod.

'When you're ready, attach the grappling hook itself.'

This was a hefty black, spring-loaded device with three curved arms, each ending in a hook. Once it was in place, Jake pointed to the house. 'You want to land that thing on the roof, right at the point we were abseiling from. You ready?' He adjusted it in her hands slightly. 'Hold it like this, feel the weight. It's got a bit of a kick so pull that stock hard into your shoulder.' Then he stepped back. 'And make sure you're not standing on your rope.'

Amy gave a quick glance down. When she looked up, there was the slightest hint of humour on Salinger's face.

'Always best to double-check,' he said. He held out a hand. 'Whenever you're ready.'

Amy held up the grappling gun, took aim and pulled the trigger.

In an upstairs bedroom of the house, a large double bed was made up, all ready for future guests. Being on the upper floor, it was rarely used and dust was showing signs of settling. Weeks passed in this room, with the only sound coming from the clock on the wall, quietly ticking the seconds, hours and days by.

That was until the glass of the window exploded inwards, showering the entire room with shards, and a small, black grappling hook slammed into the opposite wall with a loud crack, denting the plaster a microsecond before the three hooked arms shot out with a *shinggg!*

'Whoops,' said Salinger, his tone deadpan.

Amy didn't turn, she just lowered the launcher and looked up at the smashed window. Her voice was cold. 'You knew that would happen.'

Salinger didn't answer immediately. He seemed to be weighing something up. 'Did you think it was going to be easy?' He didn't wait for a reply. 'So far, everything else has been.' He began to pull the rope in. 'I'm not trying to embarrass you, Amy, but it is interesting to see you in unfamiliar territory, to see how you react when things don't go your way.'

'Interesting in what way?'

'Just interesting. From the way you handle it, it's clearly you've fired a rifle before, but this *isn't* a rifle.' He pulled the remaining slack from the rope and the wire pulled up tight.

'It's stuck,' said Amy.

'So it would seem. Here. Give this a try.' He handed her a small green fob. There was a single button on the top which Amy pressed.

Salinger gave another tug on the rope and it came free, the closed grappling hook landing safely on the grass.

'The hooks retract,' he said. 'Not just for mistakes, but once the job's done. I want my stuff back.'

As he reeled the rope in, Amy asked, 'So what did I do wrong?'

'In simple terms, you're firing a lot of weight, so you have to cater for gravity. Even bullets fall, but they're so small and go so fast, that they travel a long, long way before the fall is noticeable. But with this thing, you've got the weight of the hook, plus the drag of the rope.'

'I thought you said it was ultra lightweight.'

'It is, but even with a lightweight rope and a miniature grappling hook, it's way and above the drag that a bullet has. You can compensate by guesswork and experience, like an archer firing an arrow, or . . .' He took the launcher from her, indicating a part with his finger. 'Or you can adjust this. See here, where your scope is set? The degrees are proportional to distance. The elevation is more here than it'll be on the night, but it's the distance we need to get perfect. So, we adjust the scope like so . . .' He changed the angle of the scope's base. 'There! It should be spot on. Reload, take aim, and put that thing where you want it to go.'

Amy clicked the hook back in place and tapped the CO_2 canister. 'Is there enough gas for another go?'

'More than enough. Take the shot.'

Amy took aim and fired.

With another *Pfffttt*! and the whine of rope being pulled through the air, the hook shot forward, arcing its way above the target, only to lose momentum, fall and land perfectly on the flat part of the roof.

'Nicely done,' said Salinger. 'But it's a little harder at night.'

The phone in Salinger's top pocket began to ring.

'At night?' said Amy.

Jake nodded. 'That's the idea.' Then he answered the call.

Amy followed Salinger back to the house. As they passed through the conservatory, Michelle looked up from her book. 'Hello, Amy. How's it going out there?'

Salinger answered for her. 'She's doing fine.' He didn't give Michelle a glance, just put a hand on Amy's back, ushering her in front, and kept moving.

In the lounge, he walked to the bar and pulled up a stool. 'Two Diet Cokes.'

As Amy sat down next to him, Salinger asked her, 'You want some crisps or something to keep you going?'

'Yeah, please. Just plain.'

Salinger gave Richard the nod then peered over his shoulder towards Michelle. She was still in the conservatory, her eyes back on her book.

He moved towards Amy, his voice low. 'She knows exactly how you're doing,' he said. 'She's been watching us all morning.' Then he winked. 'Just so you know.'

Amy thanked the barman for her drink, took a sip and said, 'I know. I've seen her. Over the whole morning, the only time she picked up a book was when we started back towards the house.'

Salinger looked at Amy. Was that surprise on his face?

He turned his attention back to the bar. 'Chances are, it's innocent. Probably Galloway's way of checking up on us, but all the same . . . be careful around her. She asks a lot of questions.'

'She turned away when you took the call.'

'And?'

'I just thought it was interesting. All morning she's been curious, watching everything we do. But you take a call and she turns away. Like she expected it. Like she expected you to take a break when you hung up. I watched her, she walked back here, opened a book, and made out like she'd been there the whole time.'

'Observant little thing, aren't you?'

Amy shrugged. 'Just trying to make sense of it all.' She opened her crisps. 'The call was about the job, wasn't it?'

'What? You going to tell me what it was about now?'

'No, but I'm guessing it's not good. Michelle clearly knew about it, she guessed you'd take a break on hearing it, and you nearly crushed the phone when the call ended. So, bearing in mind what hangs in the balance for my friend, I think I deserve to know.'

Salinger turned slowly, face solid, void of emotion. 'You get to know what I choose to tell you. Get one thing straight – we're not on the same level. I'm here to get you ready, to assess whether you can do the job. If you can't . . .'

'I can.' Amy didn't waver, didn't look away. She fought Salinger's stare with defiance. 'And I will.'

'Like I said, things are different in the dark. And they're different again when it's real. I've seen soldiers panic. I've seen grown men fold . . .'

Amy nodded. She'd just about worked this out. In the background, Michelle was looking over the top of her book. She was relishing the fact that Jake was worried, that he was angry, frustrated. But the job was still on. Which could mean only one thing.

'So how tight is the deadline?'

Salinger said nothing.

'That's what the call was about. That's why you're worried. You don't think you've got enough time to train me.'

'This isn't a game, little girl. We get one chance. If you mess it up –'

'I told you. I won't. How tight is it?'

'Tight.'

'What? Days, weeks?'

Jake looked back over his shoulder, checking that Michelle was still out of earshot.

'Tomorrow night.'

Amy's confidence suddenly slumped. She whispered, 'Tomorrow?'

Salinger gave a short, sarcastic smile. 'Now you see my concern. Round of applause. Well done.'

Amy stood up, drank her coke and put the glass down. 'Then let's get back to work.'

ARTIST'S STUDIO
OXFORD

Kyle heard the familiar knock, put down the airbrush and unlocked the door.

'Alex. Careful as you come in,' he said, and returned to the desk. The airbrush was linked to a quiet compressor on the floor, barely audible above the low, grinding metal on the stereo.

Another man stepped in behind Alex. He was mid forties, well built and almost bald with what remained of his dark hair cropped short. He removed a pair of small shades as he came forward. 'I see you're working hard, Kyle.'

Kyle turned at the unexpected voice. 'Hey, Phil. I hope you're not here to collect.' He turned his attention back to his work. 'It's going to be another couple of days.'

'That's too long, Kyle. The target has been spooked. We cut that last job too fine. Fortunately, Alex made it look like we'd messed up, dumped the copy on the floor and legged it. So Galloway has the copy, but he's convinced someone is trying to steal from under him.'

'Isn't that the truth?' asked Kyle. He never took his

eyes off the canvas as he touched up the edges with a brown tint.

'He thinks someone is out to humiliate him by getting to the painting before he does – to make him seem incompetent – but he doesn't suspect forgeries. At least not yet. So I'm hoping this is to the same standard.'

Kyle did look round at that point. 'If anything, it's higher. The more valuable the painting, the more they're going to scrutinise it. Come here. Take a look.' He shifted out of the way. 'It's come out well. Ideally, I'd like another forty hours. Thirty under a low heat, then ten to settle, so the glaze cracks evenly. If it's rushed, you risk peeling – biggest telltale sign of a forgery.'

Phil stepped forward. 'Well you might be the expert, but Galloway is running the job, and he's changed the deadline. So regardless of what you'd *like*, you've got until tomorrow morning. I want this ready to go at ten o'clock, and even that's cutting it fine. It just gives me and Alex the time to drive down and prepare.'

Kyle returned his attention to the painting. 'Galloway will want it examined.'

'I don't think so. He hasn't had the others confirmed because he hasn't had a reason to believe they're fake. He's taking it as read that they're the real thing. Right now, he's feeling pretty edgy. He wants these paintings out of the country fast. My gut feeling is that once he's contacted his buyer, he'll disappear for a while.'

'You can't rush this,' said Kyle. 'Seriously. This looks good to you, because you're seeing the colours, the lines. You're looking at the picture. To me, this looks like a modern copy, as fake as a poster. It isn't finished, and it certainly won't be ready in the morning.'

'So how long?' said Phil.

Alex cut in. 'I thought you said we're cutting it fine.'

'So we'll cut it finer. How long do you need?'

'Late afternoon?'

'Out of the question. We need to be in London by mid afternoon.'

Kyle bit his lip, folded his arms and slipped into though. 'Okay. If I cook it now . . .' he drifted off. 'I suppose I can have it ready by noon.'

'Perfect.'

Kyle sat back. 'I don't suppose I'll get to see the original this time.'

'You know the situation. I pay you for the copy, and Alex because this is a two-man job. But I take the real thing.'

'Don't worry, Kyle,' said Alex. 'I'll tell you all about it.'

'Very funny.'

'What's it matter, anyway? You've got a perfect copy right there.'

'It's a copy from photographs, Alex. It's not the same. You can't feel the texture of the brushstrokes, the depth of the paint. I've got to guess. I'd just like . . . you know, to see if I'm right.'

'So long as it's ready by tomorrow,' said Phil, 'and good enough to fool Galloway, that's all I ask.'

Salinger worked Amy much harder than before. Amy didn't complain; she was totally focused on getting everything right, every time. The only other break they took was spent in the library, with a few light sandwiches, going over the security systems again and again. Once Salinger was satisfied, it was back outside and back to the physical work.

When Salinger finally announced that it was time to call it a day, Michelle was there to pick up where he had left off. She sidled past him as he made his exit and then gave Amy a warm smile. 'Things seem to be going well.'

Amy was tired, and couldn't help being a little guarded. 'You've been watching.'

'Part of my job. But Mr Galloway is very impressed with the feedback I've given him. Very impressed. So much so that he's on his way back, and he'd like to invite us to dinner so we can talk a few things over.'

'Like what?'

'Mr Galloway likes to deliver news himself. Especially

good news. But I do have something that I can share with you. Come on.'

Michelle led the way upstairs and to Amy's room. The dress hanging up in there was subtle, delicate, black and looked like it cost a fortune.

Amy asked the obvious, 'For me?'

Michelle picked up the open box on the dresser and handed it over. 'And the shoes to go with it.' She let it sink in for a moment then added, 'When Mr Galloway treats his guests, he likes them to feel special. So once you're showered and ready, if you'd like me to do your hair . . . ?'

She left the question hanging.

Amy took the shoes and walked towards the dress. She didn't like to admit she loved it. Instead, she kept her back to Michelle and replied, 'Thanks. I'll do my own hair.'

And she didn't turn until she heard the door close.

Michelle returned later, making a point of how fantastic Amy looked. And from the way she swanned towards the window, turning back to the room in a practised pose, it was clear she was fishing for the compliment to be returned.

Amy walked to the door. 'Shall we go?'

They walked in silence to the dining room. Amy had seen the room on her tour of the house, but it was different now. The window at the far end was blacked out with long drapes, which, with the low-power downlighters, and the candelabra on the table, gave the room a secret, sepulchral atmosphere. Add to this the black walls, on which paintings seemed to float in their own, private pools of light, the room felt – more than any other room in the building – a testament to Galloway's wealth.

There were four places set, and Galloway himself was already sitting down as Amy arrived. He was dressed in a stylish, open-neck shirt, cuffs rolled back, showing off the watch on his right wrist which looked as polished as the crystal glasses on the table. He was clean-shaven, and the smile on his face was relaxed and welcoming.

He didn't rise, but opened his arms slightly, as he said, 'Amy. Come on in. Please, take a seat.'

Amy took careful steps, feeling the click of her heels on the polished floor. As she sat on the seat opposite, Galloway said, 'You must be shattered. I hear Jake has been working you pretty hard.'

Michelle sat down next to her. The other place, the seat next to Galloway, was empty.

'Is Jake coming too?'

'No,' said Galloway. 'No. Jake doesn't enjoy socialising. At least, not in this manner.'

Amy maintained her composure, managing to keep a slight feeling of disappointment firmly under lock and key.

Galloway continued. 'Jake's strictly hands on. Does the job and takes the money kind of man. Personally, I think your progress deserves celebration. And that's what this is, Amy. It's a way of putting my cards on the table. But first of all, let's get our starters.'

Without any obvious signal, the door opened and Richard came in with a small trolley.

He placed a dainty plate before each diner with a small salad of seared scallops balanced on a superbly artistic pallet of king prawns.

Amy's instinct was to say, 'Wow!' but she managed to control her reaction, thinking once again to what her father had said about captors: it's the ones who try to befriend you that you really need to worry about. She settled for a simple nod of approval.

'Our Alice is something special, isn't she?' said Galloway. 'She plays a belter on Christmas Day. Plenty of time for things like that, though. At least I hope so, Amy, because I'm hoping that after this little job, you might consider working with us further.'

As he spoke, he poured wine for himself while Michelle poured water for Amy and Richard withdrew from the room.

'Bearing in mind the unfortunate circumstances you came to be with us,' added Galloway, 'I know this is a lot to ask. However, following discussions with Mr Salinger, I think it's certainly worth making you a small offer.'

'Offer?'

'When I first met you, Amy, I had the inkling you were something special. Jake has verified this. He's not one for handing out praise, but he's made it clear to me that in his professional opinion, you are incredible, and certainly capable of doing the job in hand.'

Once again, Amy was drawn to the other place, all set with cutlery, crystal glass, but no diner.

Galloway smiled. 'Ah, yes. Our missing guest. That's really what I'm offering.'

Amy paused, not daring to eat.

'If you complete this job, Amy May, I'll reconsider my plans for your friend. For Mia. I'll bring her here.'

Amy blinked. 'What?' She could barely believe what she was hearing. 'You'll . . .'

'I can't let her go – at least not yet. But I can bring her here. Right now, she's safe. As promised, I've had her moved from that deplorable place to my own town house. She's there, and she's comfortable, clean, safe, but I think she'd much rather be here, with you, until we can move to the next stage. I'm sure you would prefer that too. And while Michelle and I hammer out a believable solution, the two of you can be together. You can use the facilities, train, keep fit, watch TV – it's better than her being locked in a tiny town house and you sitting around here worrying, isn't it?'

Amy couldn't hide her suspicion. 'What's the catch?'

'I believe in paying people for their skills, Amy. There is also the fact that I'm putting a lot of faith in you. You've already had the opportunity to walk out of those gates. Tomorrow night you'll be as free as a bird. But if you come home with the goods, I'll repay your loyalty.' He made a point of looking to the empty place at the table. 'Tomorrow night you'll be working. But I'd like you to look ahead to Wednesday evening when all four of us will be dining – Mia included.' He put his elbows on the table and interlocked his fingers. 'And when we do come together, I may have a further proposal for both of you.'

'Like what?'

'I think that's something I'd like to discuss when the two of you are reunited.'

Next to her, the voice of Michelle took her by surprise. 'How are the scallops?'

Amy looked down. She'd picked at a king prawn, but nothing else.

'I think Amy's taken aback by my offer,' said Galloway, finally dropping his eyes and taking a bite himself. 'How are yours, Michelle?'

'Perfect. As always.'

Amy felt inclined to try, but she didn't comment. She was too preoccupied with what Galloway had said. Finally, she asked him, 'What's to stop Mia just walking out of here. You gave me the code to the gates. We could both go.'

'Well, I'd rather not resort to anything as crass as tags. Ideally, I'd like to think we can make an agreement on faith. The important thing is she'll have a lot more freedom than her current location until we can think of a way forward for us all. But think it through. Enjoy the meal.'

And next to her, Michelle added, 'And as you eat, just think, the night after tomorrow, Mia will be eating with us.'

Regardless of what they offered her, whether it was tea, hot chocolate or sandwiches, nothing made Mia feel completely safe. There were uniformed officers, there were locks on the door and CCTV cameras. And of course, she knew the chances of the station being stormed by Ed, Marge or Andy Galloway were zero, but even so, Mia did not feel safe.

She had sat for nearly forty minutes in a small room with a sofa and two chairs, desperately tired, but incapable of closing her eyes.

The door opened and a man entered, followed by a woman who closed the door behind her. The man was in uniform, the woman in smart, plain clothes.

'Good morning, Miss Cooper,' said the man. 'I am Chief Inspector Langley; this is my colleague, Detective Sergeant Brooke. First off, let me assure you that we're in the process of arranging transport to get you back home, back to your family. But before you leave us, we'd like to get as much information as possible in order to move things forward, make the relevant arrests, and find your friend, Amy.'

Mia blinked. Part of her had hoped Amy had escaped too, that she'd be in another police station, elsewhere in the country. So why had she managed to escape and Amy had not?

'There's two ways you can help us,' said the woman. Her voice was low, friendly. 'You can tell us everything you can, which will give us a great start, but your clothes can give us extra information.'

'My clothes?'

'Fibres, hairs. All kinds of evidence might have transferred to your clothes, your shoes. We'll sort out a change of clothing.'

'We also had a short chat with the boys who alerted us to your presence?'

Mia cut in. 'Have *they* been arrested?'

'Do you think they should?'

'No! They helped me.'

Langley smiled. 'In this case, we'll overlook the method they chose to catch our attention. However, they identified a man from an incident in the underpass. One said you scratched his face.'

'He was trying to take me back.'

'It's okay,' said the woman. 'But if we swab your fingernails, that's evidence too.'

Langley said, 'We'll arrange the swab tests and a change of clothing. But right now, I'd like you to tell me everything you can remember.'

The following morning, Amy was asked to join Salinger outside on the patio. He was sitting with a glass of fresh juice in his hand, looking out at the gardens. There was a jug of orange on the table, as well as tea cups, teapot and toast.

He glanced round as she approached. 'Good morning.'

Amy looked at the sky, at the grey clouds. A slight chill in the air raised goosebumps on her arms, but she simply said, 'Hi,' and sat down.

'Good night's sleep?'

'As well as can be expected.'

'How are you feeling about the job?'

Amy had been awake since the early hours asking herself that very same question, continually bouncing from one frame of mind to another, but she answered, 'Positive.'

'Good. But there's still work to do. Beginning with this.'

He reached into the pocket of his jacket, pulled something out and placed it, with a loud clank, on the glass surface of the table.

Amy just stared at the pistol. 'What's this?'

Salinger sat back and folded his arms. 'Is that a rhetorical question? I got the impression from Galloway that you might recognise it.' He nodded to the gun. 'It's a 9 millimetre, semi-automatic pistol.' He waited until she met his eyes. 'To be precise, it's a Sig Sauer, P226. The same model as the one you snatched so perfectly from Galloway. The same model favoured by our own special forces. Did you know that?'

Amy gave nothing away.

Salinger went on, 'They favour it for a simple reason. If you want to be the best of the best, you need the best equipment.' He gave it a slight push with the back of his fingers. 'Why don't you pick it up?'

'You're handing me a gun?'

Salinger gave a short laugh. 'Don't get ahead of yourself. It's loaded with blanks, as it will be on the night. But that's between you, me and Galloway.'

Amy touched the cold metal of the gun, but she held back from actually picking it up. 'You don't trust me with live ammunition?'

'Not at the moment.'

'So what's the point in giving me a gun?'

'To buy you time, should you need it. If you come face to face with anyone while we're up there, pull the gun and hold it steady. Someone with a gun in their face isn't likely to argue or take the chance that the bullets aren't live. You get me? So from here on, it's part of your kit. And talking of kit, before we start this morning, I'd like you to get changed.'

He reached down to a bag Amy hadn't noticed and pulled out something small, slick and black. For a moment, she thought it was the dress from last night, then noticed the material itself and the legs dangling down.

'What's that? A catsuit?'

'Finish your breakfast, put it on, and meet me by the side of the house.' Salinger got up, but just before he left he added, 'And bring the gun.'

Amy was right, it was a kind of all-in-one catsuit. The material stretched, but it was much thicker than lycra. If anything, it was more like a wetsuit, but with padded areas inside the thighs, arms and back of her calves and ankles and under the feet. The pads themselves were textured with hundreds of tiny rubber spikes. There were gloves to go with it, also padded, with the same textured spikes on the palm and fingertips.

Salinger was sorting out the ropes when she met him. He glanced up. 'Does it fit?'

'It feels like I'm being squashed.'

'Then it fits. Here, put this on.' He handed her a belt with fat, over-the-shoulder straps, covered in clips. 'You've a lot of equipment to carry. It doubles up as your harness.'

'I look like a spider.'

'No, you look like a pro.'

Amy reached the roof of the building with ease, the flexibility of the suit allowing for more movement than she'd thought.

In each room, there was a painting that Jake had ordered her to retrieve. These were actually blank, white canvases, but they served their purpose.

Amy had to climb into each room, locate the canvas then pull out a series of tools from her belt. Working systematically, quickly – but carefully – she removed the tacks that pinned the canvas to the wooden frame, rolled up the canvas and placed it into the black plastic tube she carried on her back.

In the third room, the canvas was fixed to the far wall. Not only that, but it was behind glass, no doubt protected with one of the security systems Salinger had taught her to crack.

Amy allowed herself a small, confident smile. She had been expecting this, and she had all the tools she needed for the job.

But as she stepped into the room, the hairs on the back of her neck prickled.

The room was perfectly still.

She didn't move. The only door to the room was closed. The bed was made, the furniture was polished, but something bugged her.

She moved silently across the room and approached the painting. The first thing to do was to assess exactly how the painting was protected, then how to access it.

Without touching it, she examined the sides, then took out a small torch and a mirror, going around the edges, examining every millimetre.

The hairs on her neck prickled again. Movement, right on the edge of her peripheral vision caused an explosive reaction. She whirled round and dropped to one knee. At the same time, she let go of the torch, snatched the handgun from her hip, and took aim, just in time to see a figure, slowly rising from a hiding place in the corner of the room.

Amy fired: three quick shots.

The figure immediately ducked down, calling out, 'Whoa! Hold fire!'

Amy kept the gun aimed, waiting for Galloway to rise again.

He did so, holding his hands up in mock surrender. 'If they weren't blanks, I reckon I'd be a dead man, eh?'

'They were warning shots,' said Amy. 'If the bullets were live, they'd have just missed your right shoulder. Right now, I'm aiming at your face.'

Galloway's expression faded from respect to anger. He clicked the walkie-talkie in his hand. 'Okay, Jake. You win.'

'This was a test?'

Galloway took a step closer. 'I'm putting a lot of trust in you, Amy May. I need to know you're really as good as my man says. In about nine hours, you're doing this for real. So put your gun away, and show me how quickly you can get that painting free.'

FARRINGDON
LONDON

Late afternoon, and Alex Crow was in the back of a van, pulling on a pair of brown overalls.

'Don't you think overalls look a bit stupid with a shirt and tie?'

Phil was opposite, pulling on his own pair. 'That's the point. If you look like a worker, people ask questions: Who are you? What are you doing here? What are you *supposed* to be doing? But if you go in wearing clean overalls, tied neat at the waist and an open neck flashing a collar and tie, they know instantly that you're management. It makes workers edgy; they think you're the one checking up on them. The only problem we have is the foreman. If he comes over, let me do the talking. You go off and examine some of the work up close: wiring, lighting, any old thing.'

'And what will you say?'

'I'll think of that at the time. For now, we just need to get in.' He clipped an ID badge on to his breast pocket. 'No one ever checks these things, but if they aren't there, it shows.' He picked up a black briefcase. 'This adds to the illusion that we're management. No one will suspect what we've really got in here. And finally, just to make absolutely clear that we're from an office and not the kind of workmen who'd ever get their hands dirty . . .' he picked up a shiny yellow safety helmet and placed it on his head.

Alex frowned. 'I thought you said it was just a refit going on up there.'

'It is. The only people who wear safety helmets when they visit a refit are architects and management. If this doesn't keep the workforce at bay, nothing will.'

Alex nodded. 'Clever. And of course, it's got the advantage of covering your face from CCTV cameras.'

'Precisely. The place will be full of them. Let's go.'

Phil pulled open the door and stepped out into the light rain.

Alex pulled his helmet down and followed. Both kept their eyes on the ground, neither looking up nor around until they walked through the foyer of the Ellison-Price building.

The lobby was spacious, with leather sofas, a large reception desk, people in suits coming or going, drinking coffee, locked in conversation.

As they walked across the marble tiles, Phil paused for a moment, made out to check his mobile phone and briefly turned back on himself. But his eyes weren't on his phone, they were checking the walls, and the corners where the walls met the ceilings. Satisfied, he continued towards the elevators. The security guard didn't give them a second look. They walked inside and the elevator doors closed.

As the elevator moved, Phil asked, 'How many cameras did you spot?'

'Four.'

'Me too. Judging from their positions, it's going to be impossible to avoid them all, and we don't have time to hunt for the hard drives if we're recorded.'

'So it's a case of keeping our heads down to hide our faces, is that it?'

'Pretty much.'

The elevator stopped at the seventh floor and the doors opened. To the right, a set of double doors leading into the office space were open and from inside came the echoes and bangs of workmen laying cable, fitting shelving units and partition walls. To the left were toilets. But there was also a single door in between the two sets of elevator doors with a small sign at eye level: 'Elevator Maintenance. STRICTLY NO ADMITTANCE.'

Amy unclipped her seatbelt as Jake parked the car.

'It's hard to take in,' she said. 'This whole thing is relying on just the two of us.'

'That's the point,' replied Jake. 'Only you, me and Galloway know where we're going, and what we're after.'

And Michelle, thought Amy.

Jake got out and grabbed his holdall. 'Time to go.'

The Ellison-Price building was a sight to turn heads: pale grey stone in monstrous, vertical columns, the glass between almost seamless and spotlessly clean, stretching up, reflecting a late afternoon sky of dark, threatening clouds. Amy had never seen anything like it, and couldn't shake a slight feeling of dread. It was one thing climbing, abseiling and breaking in through windows in Galloway's house, but this was something else.

'Don't stare,' said Salinger. 'Look down if it makes it easier.'

'Where's the second building?'

'Just behind this one. Keep walking.'

Where the target building was impressive, the second building looked shoddy and cheap. It had ugly, black, textured brick and panes of tinted brown glass running horizontally on each floor. The distance between the two buildings was the same Amy had trained with at the house, but here, looking up, and seeing the space she'd have to cover made her stomach tighten. A slip at the house would have resulted in a broken leg, but here it would mean certain death. The ground area between the two buildings was a quiet back street with no shops, fly-postered walls and litter.

This is where she'd land if she fell.

'How do we get inside?'

'The security in that building isn't anything like Ellison-Price. Half the reason we chose it. This is basically bottom of the range office space. Cheap and cheerful. All you need is a security key, which every person working in there has.'

'And how do we get one?'

Salinger produced a key. 'Galloway's resources stretch far and wide.'

'What about security cameras, alarms?'

'Like I said, this is cheap office space. If you want to fit an alarm in your own office, fine. If you want a secure building with bells and whistles, go someplace else and pay a premium rate. The only obstacle is getting access to the roof. That just takes a crowbar and a bit of muscle. And I've got both.'

The maintenance room was small. Pipes and cables ran up the back wall. To either side, large cage doors gave access to the elevator chutes. On the ground were various pieces of filthy equipment that could double up as seating.

'We're probably going to be here for the next few hours,' said Phil. 'So find yourself a spot.'

In the right elevator chute, the thick, heavy cables that hung down began to shiver and shake, the cage door began to vibrate, getting louder and louder until – right as the noise reached its peak – the huge black box of the elevator shot up and past.

'And best get used to that too,' added Phil. 'There'll be two security guards on duty. They come on at 5:30, which is when the front desk goes off duty. Unfortunately, the offices don't clear until much later. Things should be quiet by eight, though. Anyone still up there after that is probably in for the long haul; they'll also be on fobs, so if they do come down, and security aren't there, they'll just assume they're elsewhere and let themselves out.

If they come down while we're dealing with the guard . . . then we'll just have to deal with it.'

'What about the penthouse itself?'

'Empty – the owner likes to entertain up there, but not tonight. So our plan is relatively simple. We take out the guards, switch the painting and get out.'

Alex smiled.

Phil looked up. 'What's so funny?'

'Just reminiscing. The first painting I ever stole, back in school. I never thought it would turn into a career.'

'Alex.' Phil tapped the side of his head. 'Mind on the job. Because there's one more thing to bear in mind.'

Alex nodded. 'Getting access to the penthouse.'

'No. That should be simple enough. The problem is the chance of meeting the other team when we're up there.'

'You think they could beat us?'

'It's going to be tight, I know that much. Their plan is to wait until it gets dark, but my gut feeling is they won't.'

'Why not?'

Again, Phil made eye contact. 'Because I wouldn't.'

ROOFTOP
APC OFFICE SPACE

Getting to the roof of the second building was fairly straightforward. The security key got them in. Salinger and Amy took the stairs to first floor, took the elevator the rest of the way, then Salinger used the crowbar to break the lock on the access door to the roof. The door led to a staircase and second locked door. This took a bit more effort, but after a few goes, Salinger wrenched that lock off too and kicked open the door.

Outside, the rain was beginning to fall. The roof itself was slick and black with pools forming up against the small brick parapet and insubstantial safety railings. Beyond was the gaping open space between this and the Ellison-Price building.

Amy took a deep breath. 'I guess this is it.'

Salinger placed the holdall down. 'Put any doubts out of your head. Fix your mind on the goal.'

'We just wait here until it gets dark?' Amy wasn't sure she could. She occasionally got butterflies before a competition, but this was different. And there was slightly more at stake.

'Galloway's idea, not mine,' came the reply. 'And it's based on the assumption that the other team – if there is one – will do the same. That's not a risk I want take. If there is a second team, then they'll already be inside.'

'What makes you so sure?'

'Because that's where I would be, hiding somewhere, waiting until things go quiet, until I was sure the offices were clear. If there is a leak, which I'm sure there is, then they'll think time is on their side, because they know our plan is to wait until night falls. But thanks to the rain, we don't have to.'

'Rain won't stop us being seen.'

'People tend to keep their heads down in the rain. They concentrate on the path before them. What they don't do is stand still and gaze up at buildings.' He checked his watch. 'It gets dark around 9:30pm. But with those clouds and a bit more rain, we'll be invisible way before then.'

Salinger took a long, slim case from the holdall and opened it. Amy instantly recognised the various parts of a high-power sniper rifle.

'What are you doing?'

'It's called belt and braces. Oh, I know you're fast with that handgun, and yes, a few blanks will buy you time, but I like to be sure. So if anyone *does* turn up . . .' He clicked the stock of the rifle home. 'Pop, pop, pop.'

His smile sent a shiver right through Amy.

Alex opened the door of the maintenance room and peered out.

'Clear.'

Phil joined him. They were both still dressed in overalls and safety helmets. Phil walked up to the doors that led into the empty office space. He checked the doors. Locked.

'The fitters have left the building.' He returned to the maintenance room where he took out his mobile phone and went through his contacts. A moment later, the phone was to his ear.

'Is that security? Excellent. I'm working on the job on the seventh floor. I'm just wondering if you can check something for me. Our apprentice just called to say he's left a compressor running up there.' There was a pause, then he continued. 'No, it's fairly silent, but I'm not comfortable with it being left on all night. Any chance one of your guys could knock it off for me? Yeah, it's just in the far corner. You can't miss it. Thanks.'

He put the phone down. 'Good to go.' He reached

down, took a hypodermic needle from the case, and as the cables of the elevator came to life, he held a small glass vial upside down, pierced the seal and drew 5ml of the colourless liquid into the syringe.

At the same time, Alex had kicked off his shoes and was readying himself with a Taser X26 stun gun.

Seconds passed. The movement of the cables became more erratic, the sound got louder and then the elevator appeared, slowing to a halt.

There were footsteps outside and then the jangle of keys.

Alex opened the door a fraction. The guard stood facing the double doors, fiddling with his keys, white shirt, grey trousers, walkie-talkie on one side of his belt, handcuffs on the other. Alex doubted that he'd ever had the chance to use them.

Walking silently in his socks, Alex took three quick steps up behind the guard, took aim, and fired.

The Taser shot out two barbed, metal prongs, delivering two hundred kilovolts to the guard's lower back. The reaction was immediate. The guards arms flew out, tight and rigid, and he fell to the ground like he'd been hit by lighting. His eyes were wide, a mixture of confusion and pain, his jaw clamped tight as his muscles locked into spasm.

Without a word, Phil came over, knelt down and injected the tranquiliser into the side of his neck. The guard's eyes flicked manically left and right, but only for a few seconds. Then they glazed over, his lids closed and his body relaxed completely.

'Get his keys and open those doors, then give me a

hand to get him inside.'

They moved the unconscious guard inside the empty office space.

'I could take his uniform,' said Alex. 'He looks about my size.'

'No time. Besides, the other guard will notice and realise something's wrong. But if you walk down there in overalls,' he glanced about, 'with that roll of cable in your hand, he'll be confused. That will give us all the time we need. Let's go.'

A short while later, the elevator doors opened in the foyer.

Alex walked directly to the desk, Phil was just a footstep behind him.

The guard looked up, but before he could speak, Alex said, 'Any chance you can let us out, mate? I think we're the last two up there.'

He dumped the roll of cable on the desk and casually said, 'Don't fancy going out in that rain, though. It's rotten out there, isn't it?'

At the same time, Phil skirted round to the guard's side of the desk.

The guard, unable to make sense of either situation rose to his feet, open mouthed, just in time to be hit by the Taser.

As Phil administered the tranquiliser, Alex suggested, 'We could sit him in his chair. You know, like balance him. Make it look like he's asleep.'

Phil shook his head. 'We need to hide him. If there's anyone left in the building, working late, and they come down, then a sleeping security guard is more suspicious than one who's simply not there. Get his legs.'

They carried the guard to the elevator and dumped him on the seventh floor with the other. When they returned to the elevator, Phil took out an automatic lock pick. He pushed the prongs into the small lock below the floor buttons and pulled the trigger. The pick made a brief high-pitched grating sound while it found the right combination, then Phil turned the lock. To the right-hand side, a panel slid open. Behind the panel was a small, black numerical keypad.

'Is that the access to the penthouse?' asked Alex.

'This is the access to the top floor. From there, there'll be another door and another security panel.'

'Can you crack them?'

Phil gave him a look like he was asking the obvious, then using an ultraviolet torch, he scrutinised the keys on the panel and answered: 'Of course. That's my job.'

Standing at the edge of the building in her black suit, Amy was a shadow against the darkening, heavy sky. Beside her, Salinger fitted the grappling hook together.

'You want to do this?'

Amy received the gun, took her time in taking aim and fired. The grappling hook shot through the rain, then arced in a steady curve to land on the roof of the other building.

'Perfect.' It was the closest Salinger ever got to praise. He was down on his knees, using the parapet as leverage to pull in the slack from the rope and secure it at this end. 'Okay, turn your earpiece on.'

Amy did so and heard a loud click in her right ear, followed a by steady, low hiss. Salinger did the same.

'How's that?' His voice came through tinny, but clear.

'Fine. How about me?'

Salinger nodded. 'Loud and clear. You ready to go?'

Amy felt a flutter in her stomach and tensed to keep the butterflies at bay. 'It looks so much further when you're up here.'

Salinger's response was cold and to the point. 'Don't think about it. Just get over there, do the job, and get back.'

Amy quietly nodded. Salinger wasn't going to shower her with praise to build her up, and he wasn't going to cater to her ego like some hyped up or over-ambitious gymnastic instructor. He was here to do a job, and so was she.

So she double-checked her carabiner, clicked it on to the rope, locked it, and leaned over the parapet.

And then she was in the air. She was in the dead space between two buildings, hanging upside down, legs hooked over the rope. The texture on her gloves, on her suit, gripped the rope like it was dry. She worked quickly, hands grabbing the rope, pulling herself smoothly, silently through the rain as it hammered on her face and body.

Frightening thoughts came from nowhere: she was tired, her arms were weakening, she'd never make it. But Amy ignored them. She kept going, hand over hand, not thinking about the distance, not thinking about the seconds ticking by, only thinking, 'One more, one more, one more . . .'

In her right ear, she heard Salinger whisper, 'You're past halfway.'

Amy didn't answer, just kept going, repeating the same words in her mind until she could see the edge of the other building.

Alex walked through the final security door, into the penthouse. The light from the elevator illuminated the foyer, but as he stepped into the main reception room, he clicked on his torch and briefly scanned the area with the beam.

'Dear God,' he whispered. 'It's like a palace in here.'

Phil was right behind him. 'Keep your light on the floor; don't look at the beam. Adjust your eyes to the ambient light.'

'It's pitch black in here.'

'Give your eyes a chance. Nothing attracts attention more than a light show. Keep your beam down.'

Alex did as he was told. At first, he could only make out bold details: a door frame, a cabinet, a vase. But slowly, the details became clear, from the statuettes in the cabinet, to the droplets on the chandelier overhead.

He gave a slow, gentle whistle. 'So this is how the other half live, eh?'

Phil stopped in front of him. 'Mind on the job, eh?'

Alex frowned. 'What's the problem?'

Phil leaned forward. 'You know exactly what my problem is. So let's just find the painting and get to work.'

Alex paused. 'Yeah, okay. Sorry, man.'

He took another glance around, then pressed on, doing his best to ignore the stench of money coming at him from all sides.

The room where the painting was displayed was huge. Behind vertical blinds, rain lashed at the windows, speckling the glass with a million beads. Inside the room were several glass display cases, each containing rare sculptures and statuettes. There was a huge, black meeting table surrounded with leather seats. The largest was in the centre, facing the windows, and behind that seat, in pride of place, was the painting.

As Phil dumped his case on the table, Alex stood there a moment, looking at the painting. It really was identical to the one Kyle had produced – the one that was rolled up in the tube in Alex's right hand. The only real difference was the age and the trifling matter that the one he was looking at was worth several million pounds more.

'Are you going to lend a hand?' asked Phil.

Alex snapped out of his trance and stepped up.

Phil set to work. He lay his torch on the floor and, using a tiny LED light to locate the switch wires, deactivated the security. After a few moments, he pulled back with a grunt of frustration.

'What is it?' asked Alex.

Phil stepped back. 'There's a secondary circuit.' He scanned the area above, below and either side of the painting. He slapped the walls, put his ear close and slapped again.

'What does that mean? We can't get in?'

'Oh, we'll get in.' He checked the wall again with a final slap. 'This wall is more like a solid brick column. There'll be a panel on the other side, somewhere in the other room. If it's not behind another painting, a mirror – something unprotected – then it'll be hidden inside a mains socket or a light switch.'

'You want me to go look for it?'

Phil got to his feet. 'No. You stay here. I'll have to deactivate it.' He handed Alex a screwdriver. 'As soon as you hear the solenoids open, remove the glass and switch the paintings. I'll cover my tracks – we can't take the risk of any evidence warning the other team that we've been here first – then I'll come back and help you finish off.'

Alex agreed, and shifted into position.

A short while later, he heard sounds through the wall. Something scraping. That sounded good. It sounded like Phil had found something.

Then there was a loud, mechanical clunk. He actually felt it with his fingertips and whispered, 'Nice one.'

He set to work, as fast as he could. Less than a minute later, the glass was off and there it was – *Arabesque* – the real thing, right there to touch.

'What Kyle would give to do this,' he muttered. Then he reached out and unhooked the painting from its bracket.

WINDOW
ELLISON-PRICE BUILDING

Amy unclipped herself from the wire, fixed her climbing rope and prepared for the next part of the operation: to abseil down to the window of the penthouse.

There was no let up in the rain as she took the strain on the rope and leaned back.

She took a quick look at the other building. She couldn't see him, but she knew that Salinger was watching her through the scope on his rifle.

She paused for a moment, focusing. Then she lowered herself down, one step at a time until she was in position, standing firm against triple-glazed safety glass. The vertical blinds were open, and inside the room was dark.

In her ear, Salinger's voice: 'Okay, secure yourself and get to work.'

'I'm on it.'

Salinger had explained that glass cutters were out. With a single pane, it would be no problem, but in this situation, the time taken to do it correctly – and safely – did not balance the speed required.

She reached into her belt and pulled out a coil of grey putty. Carefully, pressing it home with her thumb, she began sticking the putty in a large circle on the glass. It didn't seem to matter that the glass was wet; the soft putty squished and stuck fast.

From the ground, the glass columns that stretched up the side of the building had appeared seamless. Up close, Amy could see that panes were in large, square sections – just as Salinger had described.

'Designed for strength,' he'd told her, 'for safety. But they will shatter if the impact is high enough. If you use the right amount of plastic explosive, the sections above and below will remain intact. If you use too much, they won't, and you'll probably destroy half of the room too. So it's important to get it right, spread the putty evenly and wide. Once it's covered . . . get well out of the way.'

'Won't the glass shower the street?'

'No. The blast will push the glass into the room. Our main concern is the flash and the sound. People *will* notice that, and as soon as that happens, the clock starts ticking.'

Carefully, she continued sticking the putty on the glass.

PENTHOUSE
ELLISON-PRICE BUILDING

Alex unhooked the painting, stepped back, found an area on the floor to work on and placed the painting face down. He took out his pliers, got down on his knees and began removing the pins from the frame.

A sound from behind caught his attention. He looked at the windows, and nearly died at what he saw. Despite the rain speckled panes and the darkening sky, he could just make out an image of a slim, female figure silhouetted against the glass.

'Oh, hell.' He looked down at his work. He had unpinned nearly half of the canvas. He looked back at the figure and he could see her working, but he couldn't see exactly what she was doing. At a guess, she was using glass cutters. If so, then she was probably fitting a sling to hold the circles of glass as she removed them. He knew from experience that a job like that wasn't quick.

Alex reckoned he had another seven, possibly eight minutes to complete the job. So with pliers in hand, and working faster than ever, he continued to unpin the rest of the canvas.

Amy double-checked her work, wiped her hands, then she skirted the building, pulled herself in tight, and triggered the detonator.

There was a loud 'WHUMPP!' followed immediately by the crash of glass and objects from inside the building.

'Jesus,' she whispered.

She hadn't even realised she'd spoken the words aloud until Salinger came back with, 'Didn't sound too bad from here. You're good to go.'

Amy skirted back around.

Just as Salinger had said, the whole section of safety glass had been destroyed, leaving the section above and below intact. A perfect square entry point.

Amy bent her legs, sprang back on her rope, and flew silently into the penthouse.

She landed on her feet, pulled the rope in behind her, and disengaged her carabiner.

The explosion had certainly shaken the room. There were two glass display cases on this side of the room.

One was still standing, the other was on its side. The case was solid, and still intact, but the delicate, decorated glassware inside was in pieces.

Amy quickly got her bearings, ignored the mess and looked for the painting.

She got her first inkling that something was wrong when she saw the open casing on the wall right where the painting should have been.

'Oh my god,' she whispered, realising what this meant. 'Mia.'

And then something shifted on the floor.

A body? A man!

Without another thought, she grabbed her gun and held it steady.

The voice in her ear, 'What's going on in there, Amy?'

The man on the ground was wearing brown overalls, and rather than surrender, or even look flustered that he had a gun pointed at him, he lifted a hand, as if to say, 'Wait,' and slowly began to rise. With that same hand, he indicated his ear, then put a finger to his lips.

Amy held her aim. 'We've got company,' she said.

As soon as the words were out of her mouth, the man's other hand whipped round and threw something straight at her. She ducked just in time to avoid the pliers, but she didn't fire. To do so would risk giving the game away that she only had blanks.

Before she could correct, the gun was knocked from her grip and a second blow to the side of her head knocked her backwards. She hit the edge of the table, steadied and prepared to retaliate.

But the man stepped back and held up his hands. In one hand, he was holding something, but it wasn't the gun. It was Amy's earpiece.

With his other hand, he put a finger to his lips for the second time. With his thumb, he clicked the earpiece off, dropped it to the floor, and with a quick stamp, he smashed it to bits.

Only then did he speak. 'This isn't what you think.'

But all Amy could think about was Mia. With a scream, she jumped forward, whirled around, and hit him full force with her foot.

Alex was knocked back and hit the wall. His eyes flashed with anger. 'Don't even try it. Just calm down –'

But Amy cut him short with a forward kick directed straight to his face.

Alex used the wall to push himself aside and only just managed to block Amy's foot. He grabbed her leg, twisted, and pushed her back. Amy landed hard on her back.

'Seriously,' he hissed, looking her in the eye. 'Back off. You try that again . . .'

Amy kicked her legs, springing her body up, forward and back to her feet to shoot a punch direct to Alex's jaw. Alex staggered back, but Amy followed up with another, then twisted and elbowed him with enough force to knock him back several paces.

As Alex regained his footing, his expression changed as he said, 'Fine!'

He came at her fast. Amy was ready, but at the last minute, Alex dodged and switched course, rendering her block useless. She was left wide open on her right-hand side, and that's where Alex attacked, grabbing her by the shoulder, placing a foot behind her to knock her down to the floor.

But Amy didn't fall. She realised what was about to happen and threw herself into a backward somersault, landed, and before her opponent had time to react she snap-punched him once in the side of the head, stamped on the back of his knee and as he turned to defend himself, she side-kicked with everything she had.

Alex staggered backwards, but he didn't fall. He shook himself, spat on the floor and gave Amy a nod that was something between respect and actual enjoyment.

'Nice.'

Amy could only stare. Who *was* this psycho?

He actually smiled as he added, 'I was told you were good. I didn't expect you to be that good.'

She noticed his eyes, wide and wild and grey. If he wasn't trying to kill her, he'd be almost handsome. But right now, he was standing between her and the job. She threw another punch at his face. Not only did he block it, but he was ready for her left hook. He caught her wrist, twisted it tight and pulled her close.

'Enough! Seriously, stop.' He was panting right in her ear, out of breath, but holding her firm. 'The name's Alex,' he said. 'And you are Amy. Amy May.'

Amy frowned. 'What?'

Alex released his grip, pushing her away. 'It's all right. I know who you are. And I know why you're here.'

The next voice came from the shadows. 'And so do I.'

A figure stepped out of the darkness. Like the other, he was wearing brown overalls. As he walked forward, he removed his yellow safety helmet.

'How you doing, Amy?'

Amy's eyes widened.

'Dad?'

ROOFTOP
APC OFFICE SPACE

On the roof of the other building, Jake followed the action through the scope. It was all he could do now that the communication was down. He had heard Amy say that she had company, and he'd seen bits of what looked like a fight.

So far things had been happening too fast to take a chance, but right now it seemed the fight was over, and another figure came into play.

He was walking slowly. He didn't appear armed, but he clearly had Amy's attention.

Jake held the rifle firm, holding the figure dead centre in his sights.

Behind a murderous grin, he whispered, 'Gotcha.'

Amy stared for a moment, hardly able to believe her own father – her dad – was here, now, walking towards her. Before she could make sense of it, another, more immediate thought hit home.

She leapt forward with a scream: 'Get down!'

She hit her dad in the chest, knocking him back just as a window exploded inwards, showering shattered glass across the room.

Phil twisted round to land on his side and rolled, fast, towards the protection of the wall that stood between the columns of glass. As he did this, he called out, 'Get down, Alex. Stay out of sight.'

Alex hit the floor and scrabbled to the same side of the room. 'What the hell was that?'

'Sniper,' replied Phil. He looked at Amy. 'His name's Jake Salinger. Isn't that right, pet?'

'He's my back-up,' she said. 'He's there to stop anyone who gets in my way.' And right now, he'd be holding a steady aim, ready for anyone who might appear in his sights.

'It's going to be okay, Amy. I know all about Galloway, and I know the hold he's got over you.'

'What?'

'I know about Mia. And I can tell you, she's –'

THUD!

The noise came from the floor near the shattered window. A chunk of wooden flooring splintered as the bullet ricocheted and hit the far wall. Amy jumped.

Alex yelled out, 'He's still firing.'

Phil called back, 'He's taking pot-shots, making sure we know he's there. We need to get a move on.' Phil nodded towards the far side of the room. 'See that tube over there on the floor?'

Amy followed his line of vision. She also noticed that right next to it was a face-down canvas almost unpinned from its wooden frame. *Arabesque.*

'We're here to replace the painting with the one in that tube.'

Amy's brow creased as she tried to make sense of this.

Phil inched closer. 'No time to explain, Amy. I want you to complete the job you came here to do, but make sure you take the one from that tube, not the one on the floor.'

Amy looked again at the face-down painting, the one Galloway wanted so badly, the one that would guarantee Mia's passage to the main house. 'How did you know I'd be here?'

'I can tell you everything when I catch up with you, but right now, I need you to get that painting and get it back to Galloway.'

'But Mia . . .'

'Mia's safe.'

THUD. Another pot-shot. Another chunk of floor splintered up.

'Safe? She can't be. Galloway's got her locked up.'

THUD! THUD!

'Still firing!' called Alex, a song in his voice. Amy stared at him and he grinned back.

'It's Salinger,' said Phil. 'He's trying to flush us out.' He looked back at Amy. 'You need to move. Prove to your back-up that you're still in control.'

'She's got a gun,' said Alex. 'It's over there.'

Phil looked over. 'Loaded with blanks, eh?'

Amy frowned. 'How did you . . .'

'Never mind. Just get over there and get it. But make it look good. I'll tell you everything later. Right now, you need to convince Salinger that you're in control. Go!'

ROOFTOP
APC OFFICE SPACE

Salinger's frustration was eating away at him. Where was the girl? Where were the others? And where was the painting?

He swapped from scope to naked eye and back again, hoping to catch anything that would give away their position.

He prepared to fire another shot, but just as he put pressure on the trigger, he saw her.

Amy was on her feet. She leapt across the room and landed in a tight break-fall. As she rolled on to her feet and turned, he saw that she had something in her hands.

She was holding the gun.

'Good girl,' he growled. 'Now fire that thing.'

'Good job,' called Phil. 'You're doing fine. Now take aim, like you're threatening us, then take couple of shots. Make Salinger think you've done your bit. Ready?'

Amy pointed the gun at her dad's chest and released the safety.

Then she paused. 'I don't think I can.'

'Just fire it, Amy. If Salinger thinks you've scared us off, he'll stop taking pot-shots.'

Amy held the gun steady, but she couldn't pull the trigger. There was something about aiming that thing at her own dad that blocked all reason.

'Do it!'

But Salinger couldn't know where she was aiming, could he? So she moved her aim a metre or so to the right and pulled the trigger.

She felt, rather than heard the bang, echoed with the high metallic sound of the cartridge being ejected. And she saw the chunk of floor split where the live bullet hit.

Nearby, Alex cried out, 'Phil?'

Amy just stared, wide eyed at the damage to the floor.

'Salinger said they were blanks. He didn't trust me with live ammo.' Panic crept into her voice. 'I thought they were blanks!'

On the floor, Phil glanced at the damage. He held up a hand. 'It's okay, Amy. You did the right thing.'

'Jesus,' said Alex. 'She pointed that thing in my face.'

Phil quickly spoke up. 'That's not helping, Alex. Amy, look at me. I'm okay, see? So is Alex. So don't think of what *might* have happened? Keep focused. Hold the gun still, change aim, fire again, then step back. Do you understand me? Don't nod, don't react – just fire the gun.'

Amy tried her best to control her shaking hands, made sure her aim was far enough away, then further still, and she fired once, twice more.

'Good girl. Now lower your aim like we've gone. Hold that pose; you're making sure we've left. Now walk over to where the painting is, but keep your back to the window so Salinger can't see what you're about to do.'

Amy followed his instructions. Next to the face-down canvas there was a black tube, just like the one she had strapped to her back.

'Okay, Amy. Leave the original face down on the floor.'

'The original?'

'Inside that tube is a copy. And that's the one you're going to take back. Be careful to hide your movements. Take it out and transfer it to your own tube.'

Amy paused. 'If Galloway realises this is a copy . . .'

'He won't. And I told you. Mia is safe. She's back home, with her family.'

'Home? How can she be home?'

'Amy.'

'He told me, he's got her in some house . . .'

'Amy. Listen to me.'

'If I don't give him the *real* painting . . .'

'He's lying. *Listen*. Keep your head down but listen.'

Amy took a deep breath, swallowed, and gave the slightest nod.

'Good,' he said. 'Now, do you trust me?'

Amy looked back at the tube, the painting and the total mess surrounding it. 'Of course I do.'

'Then take my word for it. Mia is safe. She got away. But right now, I need you to focus. The painting in that tube is a perfect copy. It's certainly good enough to fool Galloway and it *must* get back to him. I'm sorry, love, but right now I can't say any more than that. Once it's in his hands, he'll take off and I'll come get you.'

Sudden panic gripped her and she clawed for reason. 'Why don't you take me with you? If Mia is safe, I don't have to go back. You can take me with you now.'

'I'm sorry, Amy, but I can't. Believe me, I want this over as much as you do. I want you safe and as far away from Andy Galloway as possible, but you've come this far on your own. All you need is to deliver the painting and I'll come and get you. If I didn't think you could do it, if I didn't think he'd be convinced by the copy then I'd take you out of here right now. But you've got an important job to do, and you *can* do it. Do you remember what I always told you?'

Amy whispered, 'Be the best.'

ROOFTOP
APC OFFICE SPACE

Salinger kept watch, a silent statue as the rain continued to hammer down.

Amy had her back to him, but he could see that she was working furiously. Every now and then, her head looked to her left. From what he could make out, it looked like the other thieves were either dead, or they'd done a runner, and that Amy was keeping a close eye in case they returned.

'Just grab the thing and go,' he whispered.

He knew she had to untack the thing from its frame, roll it and stash it in the tube, but it seemed to take so long.

'Come *on*!'

Finally, she appeared at the window and stepped on to the ledge.

'Good girl.'

As she made her way back, Salinger kept the window in his sights. If anything so much as moved in there, he was going to fill the whole floor with bullets.

Seconds passed.

The girl came closer, arms working quickly.

Salinger checked the scope. The room remained still.

Amy landed on the roof next to him. She was out of breath, and she looked shaken up.

Salinger rose to his feet, holding the rifle by his side, and aimed the long barrel directly at Amy. Amy's eyes widened and she stopped rigid. 'What are you doing?'

'Have you got the painting?'

'I've got it.'

'Good. But before we go any further, hand over the gun. Do it slowly. I'd hate to tell Galloway I'm driving back on my own.'

Amy reached for the gun. 'Don't you have anything else to say?'

'Like what?'

'How about, good work, well done, nice job? Thank you for putting the competition out of business.'

'We're not out of the woods yet.'

Carefully, holding the gun by the butt, she held it out. 'You told me they were blanks.'

'Galloway told me you didn't have it in you to fire a real gun. Now you do. So congratulations, you shot a man – a woman? No, didn't think so – now, put the gun down, kick it over here, and help me clear up.'

Amy paused for a second, then she placed the gun down and knocked it towards Salinger with her toe. 'So much for trust, eh?'

Salinger lowered the rifle and grabbed the handgun. 'There's no such thing, Amy. Just the job. That's all there ever is. So let's go.'

SILVER VAN
OUTSKIRTS OF LONDON

Alex sat in the passenger seat of the van, keeping an eye on the sat nav as they drove through London in silence.

Phil hadn't said a word since they'd left the penthouse. Even when they got back to the van, he removed his overalls and said nothing. He used his mobile to send a single text, then climbed into the driver's seat and started the engine.

Alex fought the desire to ask. He had a good idea what was going through Phil's mind. He had sent his own daughter back into the lion's den and it was cutting him to pieces.

They pulled into a secluded spot. Up ahead, there was a car waiting. Phil didn't move, and kept the engine running.

His phone bleeped. A text message, but Phil didn't check. He grabbed the tube and left the car.

Two minutes later, he was back. The other car pulled away. Phil turned the van around and headed in the opposite direction.

'Job done?' asked Alex.

'No. That's the delivery done. The main job is still in hand.'

The atmosphere returned and remained as they headed out of London and hit the motorway.

'You want the radio on?'

'No.'

Alex wanted to offer reassurance, he wanted to say the right thing and convince Phil he'd had no choice, but he chose to keep quiet, resigning himself to a long, uncomfortable journey.

They were still travelling north when Phil suddenly spoke up.

'Yeah?'

From his tone, Alex knew Phil was taking a call on hands-free. He had a tiny earpiece on this side.

Phil's eyes were fixed on the motorway ahead, but his expression changed very quickly from concern to anger. Then he yelled out, 'They're taking her where? What for?' A pause. 'Oh, right! This is Galloway's way of getting back at Amy for Mia's escape. Well, thanks for the heads up.'

He cut the call with a flick of a button on the steering wheel, then ripped his earpiece out and threw it aside with a yell of rage.

'What's up?' asked Alex, despite putting most of the puzzle together.

Phil's voice was so quiet that Alex could barely hear him. 'I told her she'd be okay.' Then louder, 'I told her Galloway would get the painting and go.'

Carefully, Alex asked, 'What's he done?'

There was a pause before Phil answered, 'It's what I've done that's the problem. I sent her back there.' He banged the steering wheel with the ball of his palm. 'What was I thinking? I sent her to finish a job she should never have been involved with in the first place.'

'Is she all right?'

Phil bit his lip. 'No. Galloway's taking her to Morocco to meet his buyer.'

'Why? What for?'

'He wants rid of her. He's going to make her part of the deal. He's going to sell her.'

Alex shut up, not sure how to approach this. Eventually, he was forced to say something.

'You didn't have a choice, Phil. If you'd brought her with us, you'd have blown the whole thing wide open.'

'No.' Phil shook his head. 'No, I had a choice all right. I had a choice between saving my daughter and nailing Galloway.'

'You didn't. He put her in that situation because he knew she'd succeed. And from what I saw up there, I'm not surprised. But he's trying to sell her . . . with the paintings. Think about it.'

Phil kept his eyes on the road. A moment later, he glanced at Alex. When he returned his eyes to the road, he said, 'It's the idea of what he's doing that riles me. But fine. If that's the way he wants to play it, there's only one way to finish this.'

He hit the accelerator hard.

PRIVATE AIRFIELD
NORFOLK

Galloway's cars drove to a remote airfield where a small private jet was waiting.

Amy had been dragged, kicking and screaming into the car, and was now being forced up the steps to the plane.

Inside, Salinger pushed her into a seat.

She snapped her head up. 'I don't suppose you care that I forgot my passport.'

'Very funny,' said Salinger, dumping himself next to her.

'So much for trust,' she said. Galloway had stepped onto the plane. Amy raised her voice, making sure he could hear her rant. 'I work with you, train solid, follow every single instruction and get this?' She lifted her hands, pulling the handcuffs on her wrists tight. She directed her next words right at Galloway himself. 'You made me a *promise*!'

Galloway came over. It was the first time he'd acknowledged her since their return.

'I've had more than my fair share of problems these last few days. You, and your little friend, have only added to them.'

Amy screamed at him. 'What are you talking about? I did the job! I did what I was told.'

'But your so-called *friend* didn't. I guess she put her own well-being far above yours.'

Amy dropped her hands, defiance still burning in her eyes. 'She got away.'

'What she did, is put herself first. She didn't give you a second thought. All she had to do was sit quiet and play this thing out. But no. Teenage girls have an annoying habit of thinking for themselves. In short, little girl, you cannot be trusted.'

Galloway turned away.

Amy looked down at her cuffs, but despite what Galloway had said, she didn't feel betrayed. Mia was free. That was the important thing. Betrayal didn't come into it. Rather than sit there and take it, she'd fought back and driven a thorn right through Galloway's side.

She looked out through the window, wondering about her own rescue. Her dad had been convinced that Galloway would take off, leaving her behind. But he'd known about Mia, that she'd escaped. Had he not even suspected a trap?

And Salinger. Sitting there, right next to her. From mentor to jailer in a matter of hours.

With cold sarcasm, Amy turned to him. 'I don't suppose there's an in-flight movie.'

Salinger snorted a laugh, leaned his chair back and closed his eyes. Amy gave him a glare, then turned back to the window. Down below, people seemed to be unloading the cars with increased haste.

Sudden shouts and calls from below grabbed her attention. The men down there were rushing with the last few things, calling out to each other. And then she saw it. On the polished black surface of one of the cars there was a clear flash of blue. Then another. Seconds later, the same blue flashes were reflecting off the other cars. Amy twisted round to see a whole fleet of flashing blue lights in the distance.

Police! And they were racing this way.

Had her dad realised? He must have. Or Mia. Of course, she'd have been interviewed. She'd have given descriptions of everything, the journey, the house, the grounds . . . even his name. No wonder Galloway was panicking!

But the engines were already on. The plane was starting to move, to turn. Down below, doors slammed shut and the cars shot off into the night.

Amy could hear the sirens now. They were closer, speeding this way . . . only seconds away!

The jet engines roared, and Amy felt herself pushed back in her chair as the plane accelerated, pushing faster, faster, until she could feel the steep incline. They were off the ground. They were in the air.

Her heart was pumping, her brain firing off thoughts, panic, hope, fear.

She clung on to one single thought: Wherever he was taking her, Galloway wanted her alive.

PRIVATE AIRFIELD
MOROCCO

The sun was low when they landed, but there was already a close heat to the day. She had been to Egypt a few years ago, and recalled that same feeling. In North Africa, days began with a slow, warm yawn, preparing for a long, hot and uncomfortable day.

'Take her to the car,' said Salinger as they stepped onto the tarmac.

The cars weren't quite the same spec as Galloway's long, executive saloons, but they were certainly big enough. When they had rolled out of the factory they were probably top of the range, but the angular bodywork gave away their age, and it looked as though you could write your name in the fine film of dust that covered the paintwork.

Inside, the combined smell of stale smoke and sickly air fresheners made Amy want to gag. Salinger must have felt the same way, as the first thing he did was wind down the window fully. Amy caught sight of Galloway shaking hands with a tall man in a full-length robe. She was certain she knew the correct name for that thing, but cast those thoughts away to concentrate on what they were saying.

'Any problems?' Galloway asked.

The tall man shook his head, but he looked worried. 'We need to get you out of the airport quickly, Mr Galloway. Just to be on the safe side. My driver will take you straight to your villa.'

'What about the meeting? Did you bring it forward?'

The tall man shook his head, his face full of apology and growing concern. 'Mr Alhazred has agreed to bring the meeting forward, but not today.' He held up two fingers. 'Two days.'

'What?'

'Please, we should go. We shall talk in the villa.'

The journey was uncomfortable as they travelled along long, featureless roads. In the car with Amy was Salinger, three bodyguards and the driver. Michelle, Galloway and two more of Galloway's heavies were in the other vehicle.

The villa was out of town and appeared to be stuck halfway up the side of a mountain. It didn't take a genius to work out why Galloway might have sought a place like that – the approach was steep and winding, and the villa itself had massive panoramic views. If anyone decided to visit unannounced, then those inside would have more than sufficient notice.

Salinger marched Amy up to the house and slung her into a room. He took out a key and ordered, 'Give me your hands.'

For a brief moment, she thought he was taking the

cuffs off. Instead, he opened one and snapped it onto the metalwork of the bed. Amy stared at Salinger, straining to see a tremor of guilt, but Salinger just met her gaze and winked. His eyes said it all: *Just the job. That's all there ever is.*

Her time in the villa was slow and uneventful. She was guarded continually. Even when she needed the bathroom, Amy was accompanied. She felt cheated as well as humiliated and utterly trapped. She went over events of the heist again and again, wondering how different things would be if she'd refused to go back, if her dad had taken her with him.

She kept coming back to the same question.

Why?

Why was it so important that Galloway received that *other* painting?

She tried to think of her dad's stories, tactics he'd taught her – that there is a difference between strategy and worry, and torturing yourself with the latter is wasted time, wasted thought and wasted energy. Worry can consume you, and in that frame of mind, opportunities can be missed.

So she closed her eyes, imagined a plain white screen, and pushed the worry away.

On the second morning, just as she was finally getting used to sleeping with one hand locked to the side of the bed, Amy was awakened by a hard shake.

'Time to get up,' ordered the current bodyguard.

From the conversations outside and the bustle of

activity, it was clear that today was the day of the big meeting, but what role she was going to play in all of this remained a mystery.

Amy had only been given the most basic of food during her stay at the villa – couscous, vegetables and black tea. This morning brought a change. Michelle came in, asked that her handcuffs be removed, and placed down a tray with croissants, yogurt and fresh fruit juice. Next to her another guard was carrying folded clothes.

'What's this?' asked Amy, not even bothering to meet Michelle's eyes. 'Is it my birthday already?'

'We're meeting the buyer today.' Michelle waited until the bodyguard had left the room. 'So once you've finished your breakfast, I'd like you to take a shower, put on these clothes, and make yourself presentable.'

'And if I refuse? I seem to remember Mr Galloway promising to release Mia when I got back. Instead, I'm thrown in a car, brought here and asked to play maid. I don't think so.'

Michelle's face tightened. 'It's quite simple, Amy. We're a long way from home, and pretty much in the middle of nowhere. If Mr Galloway doesn't think you'll play ball, you won't even make it to the car. You will be shot and buried. So, would you like to take a shower after your breakfast, or should I tell our men to start digging a grave?'

Amy sat down heavily on the bed and pulled the tray towards her.

* * *

There was a different, charged atmosphere on her next car journey. This time Michelle, rather than Salinger, was her companion, but Amy was handcuffed once more.

After forty minutes or so, Amy spoke up. 'I don't suppose you're going to tell me where you're taking me.'

'To tell you the truth, I don't know myself.'

Amy looked at her. 'You expect me to believe that?'

'It doesn't really matter.'

'We're in Africa. I pay attention in geography lessons.'

'Correct.'

'And we've been heading north for most of this journey. I'm guessing those are the Atlas Mountains ahead. Which means we landed in Morocco.'

'We're visiting the buyer. That's all you need to know.'

'So why bring me? Scared I'll scratch the bedpost with my cuffs if you leave me all alone.'

'Not quite. The buyer is keen to see you. Why do you think you're wearing that dress, Amy?' She gave a sly, snake-like smile. 'You're part of the merchandise.'

They pulled up at a remote settlement on a steep, rocky incline. There was one main house, a two-storey building with single level wings left and right, enclosed gardens and a low, whitewashed wall. There were other buildings, all single storey, small and square, and a few more further up the slopes plus several animal enclosures.

Amy noticed several cars parked nearby. Next to the cars, men in suits and open-necked shirts were standing guard, each holding an MP5 submachine gun. Salinger opened the car door and took a firm grip of Amy's arm.

Amy pulled away. 'What if I make a scene? What if I scream?'

'I guess you might scare the goats. But if you make things difficult, I might have to quieten you down.' He pressed a dry, heavy fist to her face. 'Know what I mean?'

Amy snatched her cheek away and looked at Michelle. 'And damage the merchandise? I don't think *our buyer* will be impressed at that.'

Salinger smiled. 'Keep joking, young lady, if that makes you feel better. Just so long as you do what you're told, then everyone will be happy.'

The main house had gardens of cacti and stone water features that were mildly attractive, but it didn't look like the house of a millionaire. If anything, it looked like a small farm.

Amy was led through the gardens, through gateposts and into a courtyard.

The armed guards followed them inside, where more, similarly suited, similarly armed men were waiting, yet the atmosphere was calm, business-like. Amy noticed that two of Galloway's guards also had weapons at the ready, but they were held casually – a token of defence rather than a threat.

When they were all there, one of the suited men walked forward. Amy noticed that he was the only one wearing a tie. He was also the only one with white skin.

'Mr Galloway, I presume?'

Galloway straightened up, and in his clear Scots

accent, he replied, 'You've got me at an advantage my friend. I was expecting to meet Mr Alhazred.'

'You will. Once you have given up your weapons.'

'Not a chance, pal.'

'Then there will be no deal. You are free to leave.'

Galloway bristled. 'Now wait a minute . . .'

'The arrangement is clear,' said the man opposite Galloway. 'And it is non-negotiable. You will relinquish your arms, every one of you, to my men. Only when we are satisfied will Mr Alhazred agree to meet. Once our business is complete, your arms will be returned and you will be free to leave.'

'No way,' muttered Salinger.

Galloway paused for a moment, then he said, 'It's all right, Jake. I get it. And I'd probably do the same. Okay. You can take our guns, and the deal will go ahead as planned, yes?'

The other man nodded. 'Of course.' He motioned to the men behind him to move forward. While half of them stayed in position, their guns aimed at Galloway and his bodyguards, the others collected weapons and did thorough searches, including Galloway, Michelle, even Amy.

Once they were satisfied, the man in the tie nodded. One of the guards entered the house. The rest kept their guns targeted.

A few moments later, the largest man Amy had ever seen stepped out from the house. He wasn't only tall, he must have weighed over twenty-five stone. He walked solemnly to a chair, and sat like a giant slug wrapped in robes. His eyes were sunken, his cheeks swollen, and his bottom lip pushed out as he spoke. 'Mr Galloway. So glad to meet you at last.'

Galloway stood his ground. 'Likewise.'

Beside him, his bodyguards tried to stand tough, looking as mean as they could, despite the fact they were unarmed and outmanned four to one.

Alhazred asked, 'You have the merchandise?'

Galloway stood straight, head held high. 'I do.' He gave a short nod to Michelle, who in turn gave the instruction to the bodyguards who had travelled in Galloway's car. They stepped forward, each with a case. They unlocked and opened the cases, revealing the wrapped items inside.

The paintings were taken, then unwrapped, examined and placed on small easels which stood on a table to the right of the buyer. Alhazred watched his men take their time in doing this and said nothing.

Michelle placed the black tube in Amy's hands and gave the simple instruction, 'Go.'

Amy felt like throwing the tube right back at her, but with so many guns, it wasn't worth the risk. When she looked up, she realised the buyer was watching her.

'Come forward,' he said.

Amy took slow, cautious steps towards him and held out the tube.

Alhazred reached out, took it from her and passed it to one of his men, but he never took his eyes off Amy. When the man unrolled the painting, he merely glanced, nodded, and looked back at Amy May. It made her feel uncomfortable, like he was sizing her up. Finally he looked past her and spoke to Galloway. 'I believe you wish to include the girl in the arrangement.'

'A highly talented gymnast,' said Galloway. 'Olympic standard. But young enough to be valuable in other ways.'

Alhazred returned his gaze to Amy. 'Quite. Does she need to be shackled?'

'The handcuffs are just for insurance purposes. If you would like them removed . . .'

'I would.'

Without instruction from Galloway, Salinger stepped forward and unfastened the handcuffs.

Amy massaged the red welts on her wrists.

'Come here, young lady.' Alhazred's voice was soft and his eyes were once again fixed on Amy. 'I will not ask twice.'

Of all of the things she'd been through over the past few days, there was something about this man's low voice and calm tone that filled her with stomach-clenching fear.

She stepped forward, dropping her eyes as she did do, all too aware that the man in the chair was studying her.

Finally, he spoke up. 'You are a thief?'

The question felt loaded, like she couldn't win. In the end, she opted for, 'No.'

'No?'

'I got that painting.' She pointed out *Arabesque* on the table. 'But that's all.'

'She did a very professional job,' said Galloway. 'Using her full catalogue of skills and abilities.'

The buyer nodded and lazily turned his eyes to *Arabesque*. 'And this painting. Is there something about it you wish to tell me?'

For a moment, Amy thought she'd misheard, or simply misunderstood. She stammered for a moment, 'It was a difficult job. We went in from the roof . . .' But the buyer closed his eyes and shook his head, a sign of utter disinterest.

Amy trailed off.

'Not the burglary, my dear. The *painting*.' He opened his eyes, sunken and dark. 'Is there something about the painting you wish to tell me?' And as he looked at her, Amy felt he was looking into her soul, as though he already knew everything she was holding back.

'I'm . . . I'm not sure what you mean.'

From behind her, she heard Galloway say, 'What the hell is this about?'

Instantly, she heard the sound of a gun being cocked. She had no doubt it was being aimed at Galloway.

The buyer sighed, then he cleared his throat and continued. 'These men have brought you here to me. They are selling you like a slave, and still you side with them. Now, bearing in mind you are no longer shackled, that Mr Galloway is unarmed and grossly outnumbered, I will ask you one more time. You may even whisper your answer in my ear, but you *will* answer me. Now, is there something about the painting you wish to tell me?'

Amy couldn't help herself. There was no way to win this game, and only one answer would bring it to an end.

She looked down and whispered something so quiet

that no one in the in the courtyard made a single sound.

But she had no doubt that Alhazred had heard, and was filled with a sudden, overpowering sense of dread that he didn't seem in the least shocked.

He leaned closer. 'A little louder, my dear.'

Amy swallowed and spoke up. 'It's a fake.'

Alhazred gave a mild, 'Ah!' and sat back.

Galloway exploded. 'What the *hell* is she on about?'

The next voice came loud and clear from the doors of the main house. 'You're ripping them off. That's what she's talking about.' And right there, on the step between the two open doors, stood the slim figure of Mia. She was dressed in jeans, a black T-shirt, and appeared to be chewing hard on bubble gum. She stepped forward. 'You're trying to sell fake paintings, *Mr* Galloway. You're selling forgeries.'

Amy stepped back so suddenly that she very nearly fell over her own feet. She turned, just in time to see Galloway's look of utter, perplexed shock.

'You? What the . . . how?'

'All three paintings,' said Mia. 'Forgeries.' She walked forward, taking a place at the side of Alhazred's chair. 'Isn't that right, Amy?'

Galloway regained control. 'What is going on here? And what is *she* doing here?'

Alhazred sat back in his chair, his eyes fixed on Galloway. 'She is here to advise me on the truth behind your deal. A truth confirmed by your own thief.'

Mia came forward, a beaming smile on her face and wrapped her arms around Amy. 'You okay?'

Amy squeezed her back. 'I can't believe you're here.' She pulled back. 'I'm so sorry . . . for everything.'

Mia lifted a hand and wiped away Amy's tears. 'There's nothing to be sorry for, Amy. I know what you had to do. And I know why.'

Salinger stepped forward. 'This is a joke. I'm not going to stand here –'

Alhazred gave only the slightest nod. A shot was fired and Salinger fell to the ground. He screamed, in pain, in anger, holding his right thigh as blood squeezed through his fingers. Michelle screamed, stepping backwards with her hands clapped to her face.

Alhazred spoke clearly. 'I do not take kindly to swindlers, Mr Galloway.'

Galloway raised his hands. 'Whoa! Hold on a second here. Those paintings are genuine. I'll prove it. I'll have them verified – unless you're prepared to believe a couple of teenage girls over me.'

'I already have an expert at hand, Mr Galloway, of a different variety. Someone who can assure me that you are not a man to trust.'

Mia whispered into Amy's ear. 'Say nothing!'

From the same doors that Mia had come through, another figure appeared. Amy's eyes widened as she saw her father step forward.

'The originals have already exchanged hands in the UK,' he said. 'Returned to insurance companies, for a very healthy payout. These paintings are copies. Like the girl says, he's ripping you off.'

Galloway's response was furious. 'And who are you

supposed to be?'

Phil continued, closing in on Galloway. 'Ah, don't worry. You don't know me.' He walked up closer, facing Galloway directly. 'And you didn't know my unit, when you sold us out in Baghdad. Remember that? The good old days, when you used to sell British intelligence for cash.'

'We've spent years tracking you down.' This voice came from a second man, who had followed Phil through the doors, who was now standing just behind him.

Amy couldn't believe what she was seeing – and from his expression, neither could Galloway. His tone was low, burning with venom. 'Richard.'

'No one more invisible than a barman, eh? And I'll bet you never knew I was in that unit too.'

Galloway pushed against the gun in his back, ignoring it to shout at Alhazred, 'This is a set up. Those paintings are the real deal and I demand my payment!'

Alhazred got to his feet. 'Enough. I assure you, Mr Galloway, I will have the paintings confirmed one way or another. And once I have solid proof,' he took a step closer, 'you will regret trying to make a mockery of me.'

Galloway looked from Amy, to Mia, and then settled his eyes on Richard. His eyes narrowed with pure hatred. His lips mouthed a simple, accusing, 'You . . .'

In a move that took the guard behind him by surprise, Galloway whirled around, snatched the MP5, turned and took aim.

Amy screamed, 'No!'

Richard, unarmed, could only stare at the muzzle as

Galloway squeezed.

Phil jumped, throwing himself at Richard as the submachine gun went off, firing several shots before more gunfire erupted, cutting Galloway to the floor.

Amy felt the world stop. Richard was on the ground. Her dad was lying across him, just as Galloway slumped backwards, gun falling, his head landing hard. Dead.

She looked back at her father, hardly able to move, to breathe. She slipped away from Mia's arms, shaking her head, unable to believe what had just happened.

And then his voice. 'You okay?'

He was lifting up, looking down at Richard, asking again, 'You okay?'

Richard groaned. He put a hand to the back of his head. 'Yeah. I think so. You?'

Phil stood, looking behind at Galloway. 'Yeah.'

Amy couldn't contain her relief. 'Dad!'

Phil looked up, but as he did, his face immediately darkened.

From behind Amy, Mia's voice was quiet, weak: 'Amy?'

Amy turned.

Mia was standing, holding her hands out. There was blood smeared on her palms. There was blood flowing from the wound in her stomach.

Her eyes, full of fear, disbelief, met Amy's. But only for a moment. A split second, stretching out for eternity as Mia slumped, and crumpled.

A NOTE FROM THE AUTHOR

I live in the North East of England with my wife and three sons.

My eldest son has severe cerebral palsy and requires 24-hour care; I work full time as a Teaching Assistant. That doesn't leave a lot of free time for family, and writing can be very demanding on free time. I try to make time when I can, writing on lunch breaks, early mornings or late at night, but there are times when that's just not enough. This novel wouldn't be possible at all without family support – especially the support of my wife, her understanding and the endless work she does with our Matthew.

So this second novel is for Paula, with thanks.

Clash, my first novel, was published by Catnip in 2011.

Find out more at my website and blog:
www.colinmulhern.com